Chills and Thrills

Chills and Thrills

TALES OF TERROR AND ENCHANTMENT

EDITED BY PRISCILLA HAWTHORNE

ILLUSTRATED BY BILL SLAVIN
AND VESNA KRSTANOVICH

National Library of Canada Cataloguing in Publication Data

Chills and thrills: tales of terror and enchantment

ISBN 1-55263-380-2

1. Horror tales, English. 2. Ghost stories, English.
I. Hawthorne, Priscilla II. Slavin, Bill III. Krstanovich, Vesna

PZ5.C46 2001   823'.087308   C2001-901372-8

The Canada Council | Le Conseil des Arts
FOR THE ARTS | DU CANADA
SINCE 1957 | DEPUIS 1957

ONTARIO ARTS COUNCIL
CONSEIL DES ARTS DE L'ONTARIO

The publisher gratefully acknowledges the assistance of the Canada Council and the Ontario Arts Council.

We acknowledge the financial support of the Government of Canada through the Book Publishing Industry Development Program (BPIDP) for our publishing activities.

Key Porter Books Limited
70 The Esplanade
Toronto, Ontario
Canada M5E 1R2

www.keyporter.com

Electronic formatting: Heidi Palfrey
Design: Peter Maher

01 02 03 04 05 6 5 4 3 2 1

Printed in Spain

Contents

INTRODUCTION

"Double, double, toil and trouble/Fire burn and cauldon bubble." What is more chilling and thrilling than witches, goblins, ghosts, and monsters? Darkness and danger, perhaps? Strange sounds and inexplicable events?

In this collection of frightening and mysterious tales, your imagination will be truly haunted. Suspense and horror mingle in a manner sure to send shivers along the stiffest backbone. The titles alone — "The Body Snatcher" and "Beginning with the Ears" — are enough to rekindle the imagination and to inspire delicious feelings of apprehension and dread.

Watch with breathless horror as Frankenstein's monster first opens his watery yellow eyes; communicate with strange beings from another world; meet a witch who enjoys nothing more than eating the people who come to live with her; enter a manor house that is haunted by a ghost; then travel to the Arctic to see a frozen, grinning corpse look you straight in the eye.

Or, if you're in the mood for something just a little less scary, read about a world of shadows in which love eventually conquers all.

These fascinating stories are told by some of the world's most acclaimed storytellers: William Shakespeare, Robert Louis Stevenson, Edgar Allan Poe, The Brothers Grimm, Italo Calvino, Mary Shelley, Thomas Hardy, Stephen Leacock, Nathaniel Hawthorne, and H.G. Wells. And each storyteller reveals a rare, imaginative vision.

Travel through the open doors, empty rooms, and strange passageways of this book and an extraordinary world will be revealed to you. You'll want to read these spellbinding, awe-inpiring stories and poems over and over.

Priscilla Hawthorne

The Devil's Breeches

ITALO CALVINO

A man had a son, who was the handsomest boy you ever saw. The father fell ill and, one day, sent for his son. "Sandrino, my final hour has come. Please behave, and hold on to what little bit I'm leaving you."

He died, but instead of working and holding on to his inheritance, the son had a grand fling and in less than a year found himself penniless. So he went to the king of the city asking to be taken into service. Seeing what a handsome young man he was, the king engaged him as a footman. The minute the queen saw the youth, she took such a fancy to him that she insisted he be her personal footman. But when Sandrino realized that the queen was in love with him, he thought, I'd better be off before the king sees what's going on, and resigned. The king demanded an explanation, but Sandrino would only say that it was for urgent personal business, and departed.

He reached another city and again asked the king who was there to take him into service. Seeing what a tall, handsome youth Sandrino was, the king engaged him on the spot. Now the king had a daughter who, the instant she saw the young man, fell in love with him and became blind to all else around her. Sandrino was forced to resign before things got out of hand. When the king, who hadn't noticed what went on, requested an explanation for the departure, Sandrino stated it was for personal business, and the king could say no more.

He went to work for a prince, but the prince's wife fell in love with him, so he left that place too. He tried working for five or six other masters; but, every time, some lady fell in love with him and he would have to leave. The poor youth began to curse his good looks and ended up saying he would give his soul to the Devil just to be rid of them. No sooner had he made the statement than a young nobleman stood before him. "Why are you complaining so?" he asked, and Sandrino told him the reason.

"Listen," said the nobleman, "I'm going to give you this pair of breeches. Be sure to wear them all the time and never take them off. I'll return for them in exactly seven years. Meanwhile you must never wash so much as your face; and never trim your beard, hair, or fingernails. But you can do anything else you want to and be fully satisfied."

At that, he vanished, and the clock struck midnight.

Sandrino slipped into the breeches and threw himself upon the ground to sleep. He woke up in broad daylight, rubbed his eyes, and immediately remembered the breeches and what the Devil had told him. Rising to his feet, he felt the breeches weighting him down. He then took a few steps and what should he hear but a jingle of coins: the pants were full of gold pieces, and the more he removed, the more there came spilling out.

He went to a city, stopped at an inn, and rented the finest room they had. All day long he did nothing but pull money out of the breeches and pile it up. For every service rendered him, he gave a gold coin; every poor man who stretched out a hand also received a gold coin, so there was always a long line of men at his door.

One day he asked the manservant at the inn, "Would you know if there's a palace for sale?" The manservant mentioned one right across from the king's, but no one could afford it.

"See to the purchase of it," said Sandrino, "and I will pay you for your pains."

So the manservant got busy and arranged for the sale of the palace to Sandrino.

Sandrino had it completely refurnished and all the rooms on the ground floor lined with iron and the entrances walled up. Closed up inside the palace, he spent his days piling up money. When one room was full, he would move on to the next, and that way he filled up all the rooms on the ground floor. Time passed, and his hair and beard got so long that you no longer recognized him. His fingernails too were as long as combs for carding wool, while his toenails had grown to such length that he had to wear sandals like the friars', since he couldn't get into his shoes any

more. A crust formed on his skin an inch thick. In short, he no longer looked like a man, but an animal. To keep his breeches clean, he covered them with white lead or with flour.

Now the king of that city had been drawn into war with a neighboring king and urgently needed money to continue the fight. One day he sent for his steward.

"What is it, Sacred Crown?"

"We are between the Devil and the deep blue sea," said the king. "I haven't another penny to wage war."

"Sacred Crown, there's the gentleman across the street who has more money than he knows what to do with. I can go and ask him for a loan of fifty million. The worst he can do is say no."

The steward went to Sandrino on the king's behalf, bowed and scraped before him, then explained his mission.

"Tell His Majesty I'm at his service," replied Sandrino, "on condition that he give me one of his three daughters in marriage, and I don't care which one."

"I will relay the message," answered the steward.

"I'll expect an answer in three days. Otherwise I'll consider myself released from all obligation."

Upon learning what strings were attached, the king exclaimed, "Oh, me! There's no telling what my daughters will say when they see this man who looks more like an animal. You might have at least asked for a portrait to prepare the girls for the shock."

"I'll go and ask him for one," said the steward.

When Sandrino was informed of the king's request, he called in a painter, had his portrait done, and sent it to the king. Beholding the brute, the king took a step backward, crying, "Could one of my daughters love a face like this?"

Just to see her reaction, he called in his oldest daughter and put the matter before her. The girl flatly rebelled. "You're

proposing such things to me? Does he strike you as a man a maiden could possibly marry?" With that, she turned her back on the king and walked off.

The king sank into a black armchair he reserved for his bad days, and sat there completely disheartened. The next day he took heart again and sent for his middle daughter, but he was prepared for the worst. The girl came in and he made the same speech to her as to the first daughter, giving her to understand that the welfare of the kingdom depended on her reply. "Well, Father," said the girl, whose curiosity had been aroused, "let me see his picture."

The king handed her the portrait, but the minute she glanced at it, she hurled it away as if she had accidentally picked up a snake. "Father! I wouldn't have thought you capable of giving your daughter in marriage to a brute. Now I know how much you really love me!" With that, she stalked off, indignant and grumbling.

The king sighed to himself. "That's that! We're headed for sure destruction. If those two made such a fuss, I can just imagine the objections of the youngest, who is the most beautiful of the three." He sank into the black armchair and gave orders not to be disturbed the rest of the day. He failed to show up for dinner, but his daughters didn't deign to ask what was the matter with him. Only the youngest girl, without a word, slipped out of the room and went to find her father. She began wheedling him, saying, "But why are you so sad, Papa? Come on, get out of that chair, cheer up, or I'll break down and cry too."

She begged and pleaded so hard to know what the matter was, that the king told her. "Really?" replied the girl. "Show me the portrait, then. Come on, let's see it."

The king pulled the portrait out of a drawer and handed it to her. Zosa, as they called her, studied it from every angle and said, "Look, Father! Do you see what a beautiful forehead is hidden under this long, tousled hair? True, his skin is black; but washed, it would be something else entirely. Do you see how beautiful his hands would be, were it not for those awful fingernails? His feet, too! And all the rest. Cheer up, Father, I'll marry him myself."

The king took Zosa in his arms and kissed her again and again. Then he called the steward and sent him to inform the gentleman that his youngest daughter was willing to marry him.

As soon as Sandrino heard it, he said, "Fine, we agree. Please tell His Majesty he can have fifty million, or better still, come get the money at once and fill up a little bag for yourself, too, since I want to show my gratitude. Tell His Majesty not to worry about providing for the bride. I want to do it all myself."

When the sisters heard of Zosa's betrothal, they began teasing

her, but she paid no attention and let them have their fun.

The steward went for the money, and Sandrino filled up a big bag of gold pieces for him. "I must now count them," said the steward, "because I have the impression there's more money here than the sum agreed on."

"That makes no difference," replied Sandrino, "if we run a little bit over."

Next he gave all the jewelers in the city an order for their finest earrings, necklaces, bracelets, brooches, and rings with diamonds as big as hazelnuts. He arranged the jewelry on a silver tray, which four of his valets presented to the bride.

The king was overjoyed, and the daughter spent hours on end trying on the jewels, while her sisters suffered tortures from envy and said, "Everything would be perfect if only he had better looks."

"Just so long as he is kind, I am quite satisfied," replied Zosa.

Meanwhile Sandrino sent for the finest dressmakers, hatters, shoemakers, and seamstresses. He ordered everything needed for the trousseau, stating that it all had to be ready in a fortnight.

Now as money works every miracle, everything was ready in a fortnight: gowns as sheer as air, embroidered to the knees; petticoats trimmed with yards of damask; handkerchiefs so full of embroidery there was no place to blow your nose; dresses of many colored silks, of bejeweled gold and silver brocade, of red and deep blue velvet.

The evening before the wedding, Sandrino had four tubs filled with hot and cold water. When they were full he jumped into the one with the hottest water and soaked until the layers of filth on him loosened. Then he jumped into the other hot tub and proceeded to scrub; the dirt peeled off like chips from a carpenter's plane. He had not bathed for seven years! When the heaviest layers of dirt were gone, he jumped into another tub, this

one full of perfumed water just barely tepid. There he lathered until his beautiful skin of former times was again recognizable. Then he jumped into the last tub containing cologne, where he lingered for some time in a final rinsing. "Send for the barber at once!" The barber came, sheared him like a sheep, applied curling irons and pomades, and finally cut his fingernails and toenails.

The next morning when he stepped from his carriage to fetch the bride, the sisters who were looking out the window to see the monster arrive, found themselves face to face with the handsomest of young men. "Who can he be? Probably someone sent by the bridegroom so as to avoid appearing in person."

Even Zosa thought it was one of his friends, and got into the carriage. Upon arriving at the palace, she said, "And the bridegroom?"

Sandrino took the portrait she had already seen of him and said, "Look carefully at those eyes, look at the mouth. Don't you recognize me?"

Zosa went wild with joy. "But how on earth did you ever sink to such a state?"

"Ask me nothing more," replied the bridegroom.

Upon learning that the bridegroom was none other than he, the sisters were consumed with envy. Throughout the wedding banquet they glared at the happy couple and whispered to one another, "We'll give our soul to the Devil for the sake of seeing their happiness end."

Now that very day the seven years set by the Devil were up, and he was expected at midnight to reclaim the breeches. At eleven o'clock the bridegroom bid all the guests good night, saying he wished to be alone. "Dear wife," he advised Zosa when they were by themselves, "you go on to bed, and I'll join you later." Zosa wondered, "What in the world is on his mind?" Still, assisted by

her maids of honor, she undressed and went to bed.

Sandrino had bundled up the Devil's breeches, and sat waiting for him. The servants had all been sent off to bed, and he was alone. All of a sudden he noticed he had goose pimples and his heart was in his mouth. Midnight struck.

The house shook. Sandrino saw the Devil advancing toward him, and held out the bundle. "Here, take your breeches! Go on, take them!" he said.

"I ought to take your soul now," said the Devil.

Sandrino shuddered.

"But since you are responsible for my finding two other souls," continued the Devil, "I'll take those two instead of yours and leave you in peace!"

The next morning Sandrino was sleeping peacefully beside his wife, when the king came in to greet them and inquire if Zosa knew anything about her sisters, who had disappeared. They went into the sisters' bedroom, but it was empty. On the table was this note: "May you be cursed! We are damned because of you, and the Devil is taking us away."

Then Sandrino realized who the two souls were that the Devil had taken in place of him.

High Beams

URBAN LEGEND

Julie left the college library late one evening after many hours of studying. She crossed the parking lot to her car, unlocked it, and put her stack of books on the passenger seat. Counting the books, she realized she left one inside the library on the check-out desk, so she closed the car door and ran back into the building.

A minute later, she came back out with the missing book in her hand. She got into the driver's seat of the car and tossed the book onto the pile with the others. Then she started the car and pulled out onto the road. She had a long drive ahead of her.

A while later, she stopped at a red light. A pickup truck stopped beside her, but she hardly noticed it. Tapping her fingers on the steering wheel, she waited for the light to change. Suddenly, the pickup truck driver honked. Julie jumped in her seat, startled. She looked around, but they were the only two cars at the intersection, so she realized he must be honking at her, for some reason. She tried to catch a glimpse of the truck's driver, but his windows were much higher than hers and she couldn't see into the truck at all.

"Why did he honk at me? I didn't do anything," Julie mumbled, annoyed at how startled she'd been.

The light turned green and Julie continued on her way. She turned onto the highway. She had almost forgotten about the pickup truck, but without warning, her car was flooded with light from behind.

Squinting into the rearview mirror, Julie could just barely make out the same pickup truck that had honked at her in the intersection. It was right behind her with the high beams on, making it painful for her to keep looking into the mirror. Then they went off, and the truck continued driving behind her with its normal headlights on.

"Thank goodness! He just about blinded me with those high beams!" Julie said to herself. But now she was beginning to get a little nervous about this strange driver behind her. They were the only ones on the highway at this late hour.

The high beams went on again. Then off.

"Forget this, I'm losing this guy," Julie decided. She stepped on the gas. But when she checked the rearview mirror again, she could see that the pickup truck was keeping pace with her. Pressing her lips together, she focused on the road ahead and floored it.

Again, another wash of white light from the pickup truck. Again, it went off.

By now, Julie was definitely scared. A glance in the mirror made it clear the pickup truck was following her, and closely. But she knew she was finally nearing home. Her only hope was to outrun him.

She pulled off the highway onto her street. She could see her house at the end of the block. Another flash of light told her that the truck was still on her tail, but she didn't look back.

Screeching her tires, Julie pulled into her driveway. She leapt out of the car and ran for the front door, almost before the car had completely stopped. She could hear the pickup squeal to a stop at the curb. Terrified now, she stumbled up onto the porch and pounded on the door in a blind panic.

"Mom! Dad! Help!" she screamed.

As the lights went on in the house, she turned to face who she was certain would be her attacker. Sure enough, the driver of the pickup truck had sprung out of his vehicle. But as Julie was about to scream again, the driver ran to the rear door of her car, yanked it open, and reached for something in the back seat. To Julie's astonishment, he pulled a man out of her car.

The front door opened, and Julie's frightened parents joined her on the porch to witness the truck driver grappling with the strange man who had been in Julie's back seat. After a long struggle, the driver managed to punch the other man unconscious.

As the pickup truck driver told the police later, he had seen the man with the ten-inch hunting knife hiding in Julie's back seat when they were both stopped at the intersection. He had tried to get her attention by honking at her, but she hadn't understood. So he had decided to follow her, hoping for an opportunity to help. And whenever the would-be killer had risen from his crouching position, knife raised to attack, the driver had frightened him into hiding again by turning on his high beams.

The Body Snatcher

ROBERT LOUIS STEVENSON

Every night in the year, four of us sat in the small parlor of the George at Debenham — the undertaker, and the landlord, and Fettes, and myself. Sometimes there would be more; but blow high, blow low, come rain or snow or frost, we four would be each planted in his own particular armchair. Fettes was an old drunken Scotchman, a man of education obviously, and a man of some property, since he lived in idleness. He had come to Debenham years ago, while still young, and by a mere continuance of living had grown to be an adopted townsman. His blue camlet cloak was a local antiquity, like the church spire. His place in the parlor at the George, his absence from church, his old, crapulous, disreputable vices, were all things of course in Debenham. He had some vague radical opinions and some fleeting infidelities, which he would now and again set forth and emphasise with tottering slaps upon the table. He drank rum — five glasses regularly every evening; and for the greater portion of his nightly visit to the George sat, with his glass in his right hand, in a state of melancholy alcoholic saturation. We called him the Doctor, for he was supposed to have some special knowledge of medicine, and had been known, upon a pinch, to set a fracture or reduce a dislocation; but beyond these slight particulars, we had no knowledge of his character and antecedents.

One dark winter night — it had struck nine some time before the landlord joined us — there was a sick man in the George, a great neighboring proprietor suddenly struck down with apoplexy on his way to Parliament; and the great man's still greater London doctor had been telegraphed to his bedside. It was the first time that such a thing had happened in Debenham, for the railway was but newly open, and we were all proportionately moved by the occurrence.

"He's come," said the landlord, after he had filled and lighted his pipe.

"He?" said I. "Who? — not the doctor?"

"Himself," replied our host.

"What is his name?"

"Dr. Macfarlane," said the landlord.

Fettes was far through his third tumblers stupidly fuddled, now nodding over, now staring mazily around him; but at the last word he seemed to awaken, and repeated the name "Macfarlane" twice, quietly enough the first time, but with sudden emotion at the second.

"Yes," said the landlord, "that's his name, Doctor Wolfe Macfarlane."

Fettes became instantly sober; his eyes awoke, his voice became clear, loud, and steady, his language forcible and earnest. We were all startled by the transformation, as if a man had risen from the dead.

"I beg your pardon," he said. "I am afraid I have not been paying much attention to your talk. Who is this Wolfe Macfarlane?" And then, when he had heard the landlord out, "It cannot be, it cannot be," he added; "and yet I would like well to see him face to face."

"Do you know him, Doctor?" asked the undertaker, with a gasp.

"God forbid!" was the reply. "And yet the name is a strange one; it were too much to fancy two. Tell me, landlord, is he old?"

"Well," said the host, "he's not a young man, to be sure, and his hair is white; but he looks younger than you."

"He is older, though; years older. But," with a slap upon the table, "it's the rum you see in my face — rum and sin. This man, perhaps, may have an easy conscience and a good digestion. Conscience! Hear me speak. You would think I was some good, old, decent Christian, would you not? But no, not I; I never canted. Voltaire might have canted if he'd stood in my shoes; but the brains" — with a rattling fillip on his bald head — "the brains were clear and active, and I saw and made no deductions."

"If you know this doctor," I ventured to remark, after a somewhat awful pause, "I should gather that you do not share the landlord's good opinion."

Fettes paid no regard to me.

"Yes," he said, with sudden decision, "I must see him face to face."

There was another pause, and then a door was closed rather sharply on the first floor, and a step was heard upon the stair.

"That's the doctor," cried the landlord. "Look sharp, and you can catch him."

It was but two steps from the small parlor to the door of the old George Inn; the wide oak staircase landed almost in the street; there was room for a Turkish rug and nothing more between the threshold and the last round of the descent; but this little space was every evening brilliantly lit up, not only by the light upon the stair and the great signal-lamp below the sign, but by the warm radiance of the barroom window. The George thus brightly advertised itself to passersby in the cold street. Fettes walked steadily to the spot, and we, who were hanging behind, beheld the two men meet, as one of them had phrased it, face to face. Dr. Macfarlane was alert and vigorous. His white hair set off his pale and placid, although energetic, countenance. He was richly dressed in the finest of broadcloth and the whitest of linen, with a great gold watch-chain, and studs and spectacles of the same precious material. He wore a broad-folded tie, white and speckled with lilac, and he carried on his arm a comfortable driving-coat of fur. There was no doubt but he became his years, breathing, as he did, of wealth and consideration; and it was a surprising contrast to see our parlor sot — bald, dirty, pimpled, and robed in his old camlet cloak — confront him at the bottom of the stairs.

"Macfarlane!" he said somewhat loudly, more like a herald than a friend.

The great doctor pulled up short on the fourth step, as though the familiarity of the address surprised and somewhat shocked his dignity.

"Toddy Macfarlane!" repeated Fettes.

The London man almost staggered. He stared for the swiftest of seconds at the man before him, glanced behind him with a sort of scare, and then in a startled whisper "Fettes!" he said, "you!"

"Ay," said the other, "me! Did you think I was dead too? We are not so easy shut of our acquaintance."

"Hush, hush!" exclaimed the doctor. "Hush, hush! This meeting is so unexpected — I can see you are unmanned. I hardly knew you, I confess, at first; but I am overjoyed — overjoyed to have this opportunity. For the present it must be how-d'ye-do and good-bye in one, for my fly is waiting, and I must not fail the train; but you shall — let me see — yes — you shall give me your address, and you can count on early news of me. We must do

something for you, Fettes. I fear you are out at elbows; but we must see to that for auld lang syne, as once we sang at suppers."

"Money!" cried Fettes; "money from you! The money that I had from you is lying where I cast it in the rain."

Dr. Macfarlane had talked himself into some measure of superiority and confidence, but the uncommon energy of this refusal cast him back into his first confusion.

A horrible, ugly look came and went across his almost venerable countenance. "My dear fellow," he said, "be it as you please; my last thought is to offend you. I would intrude on none. I will leave you my address however —"

"I do not wish it — I do not wish to know the roof that shelters you," interrupted the other. "I heard your name; I feared it might be you; I wished to know if, after all, there were a God; I know now that there is none. Begone!"

He still stood in the middle of the rug, between the stair and doorway; and the great London physician, in order to escape, would be forced to step to one side. It was plain that he hesitated before the thought of this humiliation. White as he was, there was a dangerous glitter in his spectacles; but while he still paused uncertain, he became aware that the driver of his fly was peering in from the street at this unusual scene, and caught a glimpse at the same time of our little body from the parlor, huddled by the corner of the bar. The presence of so many witnesses decided him at once to flee. He crouched together, brushing on the wainscot, and made a dart like a serpent, striking for the door. But his tribulation was not yet entirely at an end, for even as he was passing Fettes clutched him by the arm and these words came in a whisper, and yet painfully distinct, "Have you seen it again?"

The great rich London doctor cried out aloud with a sharp, throttling cry; he dashed his questioner across the open space, and, with his hands over his head, fled out of the door like a detected thief. Before it had occurred to one of us to make a movement the fly was already rattling toward the station. The scene was over like a dream, but the dream had left proofs and traces of its passage. Next day the servant found the fine gold spectacles broken on the threshold, and that very night we were all standing breathless by the barroom window, and Fettes at our side, sober, pale, and resolute in look.

"God protect us, Mr. Fettes!" said the landlord, coming first into possession of his customary senses. "What in the universe is all this? These are strange things you have been saying."

Fettes turned toward us; he looked us each in succession in the face. "See if you can hold your tongues," said he. "That man Macfarlane is not safe to cross; those that have done so already have repented it too late."

And then, without so much as finishing his third glass, far less waiting for the other two, he bade us good-bye and went forth, under the lamp of the hotel, into the black night.

We three turned to our places in the parlor, with the big red fire and four clear candles; and as we recapitulated what had passed the first chill of our surprise soon changed into a glow of curiosity. We sat late; it was the latest session I have known in the old George. Each man, before we parted, had his theory that he was bound to prove; and none of us had any nearer business in this world than to track out the past of our condemned companion, and surprise the secret that he shared with the great London doctor. It is no great boast, but I believe I was a better hand at worming out a story than either of my fellows at the George; and perhaps there is now no other man alive who could narrate to you the following foul and unnatural events.

In his young days Fettes studied medicine in the schools of Edinburgh. He had talent of a kind, the talent that picks up swiftly what it hears and readily retells it for its own. He worked little at home; but he was civil, attentive, and intelligent in the presence of his masters. They soon picked him out as a lad who listened closely and remembered well; nay, strange as it seemed to me when I first heard it, he was in those days well favored, and pleased by his exterior. There was, at that period, a certain extramural teacher of anatomy, whom I shall here designate by the letter K. His name was subsequently too well known. The man who bore it skulked through the streets of Edinburgh in disguise, while the mob that applauded at the execution of Burke called loudly for the blood of his employer. But Mr. K —— was then at the top of his vogue; he enjoyed a popularity due partly to his own talent and address, partly to the incapacity of his rival, the university professor. The students, at least, swore by his name, and Fettes believed himself, and was believed by others, to have laid the foundations of success when he had acquired the favor of this meteorically famous man. Mr. K —— was a *bon vivant* as well as an accomplished teacher; he liked a sly allusion no less than a careful preparation. In both capacities Fettes enjoyed and deserved his notice, and by the second year of his attendance he held the half-regular position of second demonstrator or sub-assistant in his class.

In this capacity, the charge of the theater and lecturerdom devolved in particular upon his shoulders. He had to answer for the cleanliness of the premises and the conduct of the other students, and it was a part of his duty to supply, receive, and divide the various subjects. It was with a view to this last — at that time very delicate — affair that he was lodged by Mr. K —— in the same wynd, and at last in the same building, with the dissecting room. Here, after a night of turbulent pleasures, his hand still tottering, his sight still misty and confused, he would be called out of bed in the black hours before the winter dawn by the unclean and desperate interlopers who supplied the table. He would open the door to these men, since infamous throughout the land. He would help them with their tragic burden, pay them their sordid price, and remain alone, when they were gone, with the unfriendly relics of humanity. From such a scene he would return to snatch another hour or two of slumber, to repair the abuses of the night, and refresh himself for the labors of the day.

Few lads could have been more insensible to the impressions of a life thus passed among the ensigns of mortality. His mind was closed against all general considerations. He was incapable of interest in the fate and fortunes of another, the slave of his own desires and low ambitions. Cold, light, and selfish in the last resort, he had that modicum of prudence, miscalled morality, which keeps a man from inconvenient drunkenness or punishable theft. He coveted, besides, a measure of consideration from his masters and his fellow-pupils, and he had no desire to fail conspicuously in the external parts of life. Thus he made it his pleasure to gain some distinction in his studies, and day after day rendered unimpeachable eye-service to his employer, Mr. K —— . For his day of work he indemnified himself by nights of roaring, blackguardly enjoyment; and when that balance had been struck, the organ that he called his conscience declared itself content.

The supply of subjects was a continual trouble to him as well as to his master. In that large and busy class, the raw material of the anatomists kept perpetually running out; and the business thus rendered necessary was not only unpleasant in itself, but threatened dangerous consequences to all who were concerned. It was the policy of Mr. K —— to ask no questions in his dealings with the trade. "They bring the body, and we pay the price," he used to say, dwelling on the alliteration — "*quid pro quo*." And again, and somewhat profanely, "Ask no questions," he would tell his assistants, "for conscience sake." There was no understanding that the subjects were provided by the crime of murder. Had that idea been broached to him in words, he would have recoiled in horror; but the lightness of his speech upon so grave a matter was, in itself, an offence against good manners, and a temptation to the men with whom he dealt. Fettes, for instance, had often remarked to himself upon the singular freshness of the bodies. He had been struck again and again by the hangdog, abominable looks of the ruffians who came to him before the dawn; and putting things together clearly in his private thoughts, he perhaps attributed a meaning too immoral and too categorical to the unguarded counsels of his master. He understood his duty, in short, to have three branches: to take what was brought, to pay the price, and to avert the eye from any evidence of crime.

One November morning this policy of silence was put sharply to the test. He had been awake all night with a racking toothache — pacing his room like a caged beast or throwing himself in fury on his bed — and had fallen at last into that profound, uneasy slumber that so often follows on a night of pain, when he was awakened by the third or fourth angry repetition of the concerted signal. There was a thin, bright moonshine; it was bitter cold, windy, and frosty; the town had not yet awakened, but an indefinable stir already preluded the noise and business of the day. The ghouls had come later than usual, and they seemed more than usually eager to be gone. Fettes, sick with sleep, lighted them upstairs. He heard their grumbling Irish voices through a dream; and as they stripped the sack from their sad merchandise he leaned dozing, with his shoulder propped against the wall; he had to shake himself to find the men their money. As he did so his

eyes lighted on the dead face. He started; he took two steps nearer, with the candle raised.

"God Almighty!" he cried. "That is Jane Galbraith!" The men answered nothing, but they shuffled nearer the door.

"I know her, I tell you," he continued. "She was alive and hearty yesterday. It's impossible she can be dead; it's impossible you should have got this body fairly."

"Sure, sir, you're mistaken entirely," said one of the men.

But the other looked Fettes darkly in the eyes, and demanded the money on the spot.

It was impossible to misconceive the threat or to exaggerate the danger. The lad's heart failed him. He stammered some excuses, counted out the sum, and saw his hateful visitors depart. No sooner were they gone than he hastened to confirm his doubts. By a dozen unquestionable marks he identified the girl he had jested with the day before. He saw, with horror, marks upon her body that might well betoken violence. A panic seized him, and he took refuge in his room. There he reflected at length over the discovery that he had made; considered soberly the bearing of Mr. K —— 's instructions and the danger to himself of interference in so serious a business, and at last, in sore perplexity, determined to wait for the advice of his immediate superior, the class assistant.

This was a young doctor, Wolfe Macfarlane, a high favorite among all the reckless students, clever, dissipated, and unscrupulous to the last degree. He had traveled and studied abroad. His manners were agreeable and a little forward. He was an authority on the stage, skillful on the ice or the links with skate or golf club; he dressed with nice audacity, and, to put the finishing touch upon his glory, he kept a gig and a strong trotting horse. With Fettes he was on terms of intimacy; indeed, their relative positions called for some community of life; and when subjects were scarce the pair would drive far into the country in Macfarlane's gig, visit and desecrate some lonely graveyard, and return before dawn with their booty to the door of the dissecting room.

On that particular morning Macfarlane arrived somewhat earlier than his wont. Fettes heard him, and met him on the stairs, told him his story, and showed him the cause of his alarm. Macfarlane examined the marks on her body.

"Yes," he said with a nod, "it looks fishy."

"Well, what should I do?" asked Fettes.

"Do?" repeated the other. "Do you want to do anything? Least said soonest mended, I should say."

"Some one else might recognize her," objected Fettes. "She was as well known as the Castle Rock."

"We'll hope not," said Macfarlane, "and if anybody does — well, you didn't, don't you see, and there's an end. The fact is, this has

been going on too long. Stir up the mud, and you'll get K ———
into the most unholy trouble; you'll be in a shocking box yourself.
So will I, if you come to that. I should like to know how any one
of us would look, or what the devil we should have to say for
ourselves in any Christian witness-box. For me, you know there's
one thing certain — that, practically speaking, all our subjects
have been murdered."

"Macfarlane!" cried Fettes.

"Come now!" sneered the other. "As if you hadn't suspected it
yourself!"

"Suspecting is one thing —"

"And proof another. Yes, I know; and I'm as sorry as you are
this should have come here," tapping the body with his cane.
"The next best thing for me is not to recognize it; and," he added
coolly, "I don't. You may, if you please. I don't dictate, but I think
a man of the world would do as I do; and I may add, I fancy that
is what K ——— would look for at our hands. The question is,
Why did he choose us two for his assistants? And I answer,
because he didn't want old wives."

This was the tone of all others to affect the mind of a lad like
Fettes. He agreed to imitate Macfarlane. The body of the
unfortunate girl was duly dissected, and no one remarked or
appeared to recognize her.

One afternoon, when his day's work was over, Fettes dropped
into a popular tavern and found Macfarlane sitting with a stranger.
This was a small man, very pale and dark, with coal-black eyes.
The cut of his features gave a promise of intellect and refinement
which was but feebly realized in his manners, for he proved, upon
a nearer acquaintance, coarse, vulgar, and stupid. He exercised,
however, a very remarkable control over Macfarlane; issued
orders like the Great Bashaw; became inflamed at the least

discussion or delay, and commented rudely on the servility with which he was obeyed. This most offensive person took a fancy to Fettes on the spot, plied him with drinks, and honored him with unusual confidences on his past career. If a tenth part of what he confessed were true, he was a very loathsome rogue; and the lad's vanity was tickled by the attention of so experienced a man.

"I'm a pretty bad fellow myself," the stranger remarked, "but Macfarlane is the boy — Toddy Macfarlane, I call him. Toddy, order your friend another glass." Or it might be, "Toddy, you jump up and shut the door." "Toddy hates me," he said again. "Oh, yes, Toddy, you do!"

"Don't you call me that confounded name," growled Macfarlane.

"Hear him! Did you ever see the lads play knife? He would like to do that all over my body," remarked the stranger.

"We medicals have a better way than that," said Fettes. "When we dislike a dead friend of ours, we dissect him."

Macfarlane looked up sharply, as though this jest was scarcely to his mind.

The afternoon passed. Gray, for that was the stranger's name, invited Fettes to join them at dinner, ordered a feast so sumptuous that the tavern was thrown in commotion, and when all was done commanded Macfarlane to settle the bill. It was late before they separated; the man Gray was incapably drunk. Macfarlane, sobered by his fury, chewed the cud of the money he had been forced to squander and the slights he had been obliged to swallow. Fettes, with various liquors singing in his head, returned home with devious footsteps and a mind entirely in abeyance. Next day Macfarlane was absent from the class, and Fettes smiled to himself as he imagined him still squiring the intolerable Gray from tavern to tavern. As soon as the hour of liberty had struck he posted

from place to place in quest of his last night's companions. He could find them, however, nowhere; so returned early to his rooms, went early to bed, and slept the sleep of the just.

At four in the morning he was awakened by the well-known signal. Descending to the door, he was filled with astonishment to find Macfarlane with his gig, and in the gig one of those long and ghastly packages with which he was so well acquainted.

"What?" he cried. "Have you been out alone? How did you manage?"

But Macfarlane silenced him roughly, bidding him turn to business. When they had got the body upstairs and laid it on the table, Macfarlane made at first as if he were going away. Then he paused and seemed to hesitate; and then, "You had better look at the face," said he, in tones of some constraint. "You had better," he repeated, as Fettes only stared at him in wonder.

"But where, and how, and when did you come by it?" cried the other.

"Look at the face," was the only answer.

Fettes was staggered; strange doubts assailed him. He looked from the young doctor to the body, and then back again. At last, with a start, he did as he was bidden. He had almost expected the sight that met his eyes, and yet the shock was cruel. To see, fixed in the rigidity of death and naked on that coarse layer of sackcloth, the man whom he had left well clad and full of meat and sin upon the threshold of a tavern, awoke, even in the thoughtless Fettes, some of the terrors of the conscience. It was a *cras tibi* which re-echoed in his soul, that two whom he had known should have come to lie upon these icy tables. Yet these were only secondary thoughts. His first concern regarded Wolfe. Unprepared for a challenge so momentous, he knew not how to look his comrade in the face. He durst not meet his eye, and he had neither words nor voice at his command.

It was Macfarlane himself who made the first advance. He came up quietly behind and laid his hand gently but firmly on the other's shoulder.

"Richardson," said he, "may have the head."

Now Richardson was a student who had long been anxious for that portion of the human subject to dissect. There was no answer, and the murderer resumed: "Talking of business, you must pay me; your accounts, you see, must tally."

Fettes found a voice, the ghost of his own: "Pay you!" he cried. "Pay you for that?"

"Why, yes, of course you must. By all means and on every possible account, you must," returned the other. "I dare not give it for nothing, you dare not take it for nothing; it would compromise us both. This is another case like Jane Galbraith's.

The more things are wrong the more we must act as if all were right. Where does old K —— keep his money?"

"There," answered Fettes hoarsely, pointing to a cupboard in the corner.

"Give me the key, then," said the other, calmly, holding out his hand.

There was an instant's hesitation, and the die was cast. Macfarlane could not suppress a nervous twitch, the infinitesimal mark of an immense relief, as he felt the key between his fingers. He opened the cupboard, brought out pen and ink and a paper-book that stood in one compartment, and separated from the funds in a drawer a sum suitable to the occasion.

"Now, look here," he said, "there is the payment made — first proof of your good faith: first step to your security. You have now to clinch it by a second. Enter the payment in your book, and then you for your part may defy the devil."

The next few seconds were for Fettes an agony of thought; but in balancing his terrors it was the most immediate that triumphed. Any future difficulty seemed almost welcome if he could avoid a present quarrel with Macfarlane. He set down the candle which he had been carrying all this time, and with a steady hand entered the date, the nature, and the amount of the transaction.

"And now," said Macfarlane, "it's only fair that you should pocket the lucre. I've had my share already. By the bye, when a man of the world falls into a bit of luck, has a few shillings extra in his pocket — I'm ashamed to speak of it, but there's a rule of conduct in the case. No treating, no purchase of expensive class-books, no squaring of old debts; borrow, don't lend."

"Macfarlane," began Fettes, still somewhat hoarsely, "I have put my neck in a halter to oblige you."

"To oblige me?" cried Wolfe. "Oh, come! You did, as near as I can see the matter; what you downright had to do in self-defense. Suppose I got into trouble, where would you be? This second little matter flows clearly from the first. Mr. Gray is the continuation of Miss Galbraith. You can't begin and then stop. If you begin, you must keep on beginning; that's the truth. No rest for the wicked."

A horrible sense of blackness and the treachery of fate seized hold upon the soul of the unhappy student.

"My God!" he cried, "but what have I done? and when did I begin? To be made a class assistant — in the name of reason, where's the harm in that? Service wanted the position; Service might have got it. Would *he* have been where *I* am now?"

"My dear fellow," said Macfarlane, "what a boy you are! What harm *has* come to you? What harm *can* come to you if you hold your tongue? Why, man, do you know what this life is? There are two squads of us — the lions, and the lambs. If you're a lamb,

you'll come to lie upon these tables like Gray or Jane Galbraith; if you're a lion, you'll live and drive a horse like me, like K ——, like all the world with any wit or courage. You're staggered at the first. But look at K ——! My dear fellow, you're clever, you have pluck. I like you, and K —— likes you. You were born to lead the hunt; and I tell you, on my honor and my experience of life, three days from now you'll laugh at all these scarecrows like a high-school boy at a farce."

And with that Macfarlane took his departure and drove off up the wynd in his gig to get under cover before daylight. Fettes was thus left alone with his regrets. He saw the miserable peril in which he stood involved. He saw, with inexpressible dismay, that there was no limit to his weakness, and that, from concession to concession, he had fallen from the arbiter of Macfarlane's destiny to his paid and helpless accomplice. He would have given the world to have been a little braver at the time, but it did not occur to him that he might still be brave. The secret of Jane Galbraith and the cursed entry in the daybook closed his mouth.

Hours passed; the class began to arrive; the members of the unhappy Gray were dealt out to one and to another, and received without remark. Richardson was made happy with the head; and before the hour of freedom rang Fettes trembled with exultation to perceive how far they had already gone toward safety.

For two days he continued to watch, with increasing joy, the dreadful process of disguise.

On the third day Macfarlane made his appearance. He had been ill, he said; but he made up for lost time by the energy with which he directed the students. To Richardson in particular he extended the most valuable assistance and advice, and that student, encouraged by the praise of the demonstrator, burned high with ambitious hopes, and saw the medal already in his grasp.

Before the week was out Macfarlane's prophecy had been fulfilled. Fettes had outlived his terrors and had forgotten his baseness. He began to plume himself upon his courage, and had so arranged the story in his mind that he could look back on these events with an unhealthy pride. Of his accomplice he saw but little. They met, of course, in the business of the class; they received their orders together from Mr. K ——— . At times they had a word or two in private, and Macfarlane was from first to last particularly kind and jovial. But it was plain that he avoided any reference to their common secret; and even when Fettes whispered to him that he had cast in his lot with the lions and forsworn the lambs, he only signed to him smilingly to hold his peace.

At length an occasion arose which threw the pair once more into a closer union. Mr. K ——— was again short of subjects; pupils were eager, and it was a part of this teacher's pretensions to be always well supplied. At the same time there came the news of a burial in the rustic graveyard of Glencorse. Time has little changed the place in question. It stood then, as now, upon a crossroad, out of call of human habitations, and buried fathoms deep in the foliage of six cedar trees. The cries of the sheep upon the neighboring hills, the streamlets upon either hand, one loudly singing among pebbles, the other dripping furtively from pond to pond, the stir of the wind in mountainous old flowering chestnuts, and once in seven days the voice of the bell and the old tunes of the precentor, were the only sounds that disturbed the silence around the rural church. The Resurrection Man — to use a byname of the period — was not to be deterred by any of the sanctities of customary piety. It was part of his trade to despise and desecrate the scrolls and trumpets of old tombs, the paths worn by the feet of worshipers and mourners, and the offerings and the inscriptions of bereaved affection. To rustic neighborhoods, where love is more than commonly tenacious, and where some bonds of blood or fellowship unite the entire society of a parish, the body snatcher, far from being repelled by natural respect, was attracted by the ease and safety of the task. To bodies that had been laid in earth, in joyful expectation of a far different awakening, there came that hasty, lamp-lit, terror-haunted resurrection of the spade and mattock. The coffin was forced, the cerements torn, and the melancholy relics, clad in sackcloth, after being rattled for hours on moonless byways, were at length exposed to uttermost indignities before a class of gaping boys.

Somewhat as two vultures may swoop upon a dying lamb, Fettes and Macfarlane were to be let loose upon a grave in that green and quiet resting-place. The wife of a farmer, a woman who had lived for sixty years, and been known for nothing but good

butter and a godly conversation, was to be rooted from her grave
at midnight and carried, dead and naked, to that faraway city that
she had always honored with her Sunday's best; the place beside
her family was to be empty till the crack of doom; her innocent
and almost venerable members to be exposed to that last curiosity
of the anatomist.

Late one afternoon the pair set forth, well wrapped in cloaks
and furnished with a formidable bottle. It rained without
remission — a cold, dense, lashing rain. Now and again there blew
a puff of wind, but these sheets of falling water kept it down.
Bottle and all, it was a sad and silent drive as far as Penicuik,
where they were to spend the evening. They stopped once, to hide
their implements in a thick bush not far from the churchyard, and
once again at the Fisher's Tryst, to have a toast before the kitchen
fire and vary their nips of whisky with a glass of ale. When they
reached their journey's end the gig was housed, the horse was fed
and comforted, and the two young doctors in a private room sat
down to the best dinner and the best wine the house afforded.
The lights, the fire, the beating rain upon the window, the cold,
incongruous work that lay before them, added zest to their
enjoyment of the meal. With every glass their cordiality increased.
Soon Macfarlane handed a little pile of gold to his companion.

"A compliment," he said. "Between friends these little d —— d
accommodations ought to fly like pipe-lights."

Fettes pocketed the money, and applauded the sentiment to
the echo. "You are a philosopher," he cried. "I was an ass till I knew
you. You and K —— between you, by the Lord Harry! but you'll
make a man of me."

"Of course, we shall," applauded Macfarlane. "A man? I tell
you, it required a man to back me up the other morning. There are
some big, brawling, forty-year-old cowards who would have

turned sick at the look of the d —— d thing; but not you — you kept your head. I watched you."

"Well, and why not?" Fettes thus vaunted himself.

"It was no affair of mine. There was nothing to gain on the one side but disturbance, and on the other I could count on your gratitude, don't you see?" And he slapped his pocket till the gold pieces rang.

Macfarlane somehow felt a certain touch of alarm at these unpleasant words. He may have regretted that he had taught his young companion so successfully, but he had no time to interfere, for the other noisily continued in this boastful strain:

"The great thing is not to be afraid. Now, between you and me, I don't want to hang — that's practical; but for all cant, Macfarlane, I was born with a contempt. Hell, God, Devil, right, wrong, sin, crime, and all the old gallery of curiosities — they may frighten boys, but men of the world, like you and me, despise them. Here's to the memory of Gray!"

It was by this time growing somewhat late. The gig, according to order, was brought round to the door with both lamps brightly shining, and the young men had to pay their bill and take the road. They announced that they were bound for Peebles, and drove in that direction till they were clear of the last houses of the town; then, extinguishing the lamps, returned upon their course, and followed a byroad toward Glencorse. There was no sound but that of their own passage, and the incessant, strident pouring of the rain. It was pitch dark; here and there a white gate or a white stone in the wall guided them for a short space across the night; but for the most part it was at a foot pace, and almost groping, that they picked their way through that resonant blackness to their solemn and isolated destination. In the sunken woods that traverse the neighborhood of the burying ground the last glimmer failed them, and it became necessary to kindle a match and reillumine one of the lanterns of the gig. Thus, under the dripping trees, and environed by huge and moving shadows, they reached the scene of their unhallowed labors.

They were both experienced in such affairs, and powerful with the spade; and they had scarce been twenty minutes at their task before they were rewarded by a dull rattle on the coffin lid. At the same moment Macfarlane, having hurt his hand upon a stone, flung it carelessly above his head. The grave, in which they now stood almost to the shoulders, was close to the edge of the plateau of the graveyard; and the gig lamp had been propped, the better to illuminate their labors, against a tree, and on the immediate verge of the steep bank descending to the stream. Chance had taken a sure aim with the stone. Then came a clang of broken glass; night fell upon them; sounds alternately dull and ringing announced the bounding of the lantern down the bank, and its occasional collision with the trees. A stone or two, which it had dislodged in its descent, rattled behind it into the profundities of the glen; and then silence, like night, resumed its sway; and they might bend their hearing to its utmost pitch, but naught was to be heard except the rain, now marching to the wind, now steadily falling over miles of open country.

They were so nearly at an end of their abhorred task that they judged it wisest to complete it in the dark. The coffin was exhumed and broken open; the body inserted in the dripping sack and carried between them to the gig; one mounted to keep it in its place, and the other, taking the horse by the mouth, groped along by wall and bush until they reached the wider road by the Fisher's Tryst. Here was a faint, diffused radiancy, which they hailed like daylight; by that they pushed the horse to a good pace and began to rattle along merrily in the direction of the town.

They had both been wetted to the skin during their operations, and now, as the gig jumped among the deep ruts, the thing that stood propped between them fell now upon one and now upon the other. At every repetition of the horrid contact each instinctively repelled it with the greater haste; and the process, natural although it was, began to tell upon the nerves of the companions. Macfarlane made some ill-favored jest about the farmer's wife, but it came hollowly from his lips, and was allowed to drop in silence. Still their unnatural burden bumped from side to side; and now the head would be laid, as if in confidence, upon their shoulders, and now the drenching sackcloth would flap icily about their faces. A creeping chill began to possess the soul of Fettes. He peered at the bundle, and it seemed somehow larger than at first. All over the countryside, and from every degree of distance, the farm dogs accompanied their passage with tragic

ululations; and it grew and grew upon his mind that some unnatural miracle had been accomplished, that some nameless change had befallen the dead body, and that it was in fear of their unholy burden that the dogs were howling.

"For God's sake," said he, making a great effort to arrive at speech, "for God's sake, let's have a light!"

Seemingly Macfarlane was affected in the same direction; for, though he made no reply, he stopped the horse, passed the reins to his companion, got down, and proceeded to kindle the remaining lamp. They had by that time got no farther than the crossroad down to Auchenclinny. The rain still poured as though the deluge were returning, and it was no easy matter to make a light in such a world of wet and darkness. When at last the flickering blue flame had been transferred to the wick and began to expand and clarify, and shed a wide circle of misty brightness round the gig, it became possible for the two young men to see each other and the thing they had along with them. The rain had molded the rough sacking to the outlines of the body underneath; the head was distinct from the trunk, the shoulders plainly modeled; something at once spectral and human riveted their eyes upon the ghastly comrade of their drive.

For some time Macfarlane stood motionless, holding up the lamp. A nameless dread was swathed, like a wet sheet, about the body, and tightened the white skin upon the face of Fettes; a fear that was meaningless, a horror of what could not be, kept mounting to his brain. Another beat of the watch, and he had spoken. But his comrade forestalled him.

"That is not a woman," said Macfarlane in a hushed voice.

"It was a woman when we put her in," whispered Fettes.

"Hold that lamp," said the other. "I must see her face."

And as Fettes took the lamp his companion untied the fastenings of the sack and drew down the cover from the head. The light fell very clear upon the dark, well-molded features and smooth-shaven cheeks of a too familiar countenance, often beheld in dreams of both of these young men. A wild yell rang up into the night; each leaped from his own side into the roadway; the lamp fell, broke, and was extinguished; and the horse, terrified by this unusual commotion, bounded and went off toward Edinburgh at a gallop, bearing along with it, sole occupant of the gig, the body of the dead and long-dissected Gray.

The Leg of Gold

TRADITIONAL FRENCH GHOST STORY

There once lived a beautiful young lady who was married to an exceedingly wealthy young lord. The lord was proud of his lovely wife and enjoyed dressing her in lavish gowns and jewels. One day, the lord came home with three trunks full of sparkling jewels and silk gowns. The lady ran upstairs to try on a gown and then, as she ran back down the stairs to show her husband, the heel of her shoe caught in the hem of her dress. She toppled headfirst down the long, polished stairs and landed in a heap of violet silk upon the floor, her leg twisted strangely beneath her.

The doctor was immediately summoned. After completing his examination, he looked very grave.

"Well, speak up man. What is to be done about my wife?" cried the lord.

"I'm afraid, dear sir, that the lady's leg is broken in seven different places. There is nothing to be done. It must be cut off," the doctor replied.

That evening, the doctor set upon his task. He sawed and cut and severed the lady's leg from her body.

"Do not worry, my dear," the lord said the next day when his

wife had woken, "I have called for the goldsmith. You will have the most beautiful leg in the land."

That very evening, the goldsmith rode to the lord's manor. After several measurements, he returned to his shop and set about creating the most exquisite gold leg ever to be seen. The handiwork was so precise that the leg fit the lady perfectly. Soon, she was running and skipping, hopping and dancing as though nothing had ever been amiss.

Seven years later, the lady was once again running gaily down the stairs in a new gown, eager to show it off to her husband. Once again, the heel of her slipper caught in the hem of her gown and she tumbled, headfirst, down the long staircase. This time she broke her neck and died.

The lord was distraught. He had his lady buried with her golden leg in the nearby churchyard beneath a beautifully carved headstone. Bolts of beautiful material were ordered from China and mourning suits were created for the entire staff. The lord's groom was dressed in expensive black satin. The groom, a handsome, egotistical fellow, thought he had never looked so elegant.

As he stood in front of his mirror admiring himself, he began to think out loud.

"What a dashing figure I make in this suit. I am far too handsome and elegant to be a gentleman's groom. Why shouldn't I be a gentleman. If only I had a small fortune..."

His eyes began to gleam mysteriously.

"Of course! M'lady doesn't need her leg of gold any longer. Why shouldn't I have it? I could sell it and set myself up as a gentleman. She doesn't need her leg anymore!"

And so his plan was hatched. That very night he threw a long cloak over his shoulders and hurried to the churchyard. It didn't take him long to dig up the coffin. He pried the top of the casket off with the edge of his shovel and then chopped the golden leg off of the lady's corpse. Then he quickly buried the lady once again. Wrapping the leg of gold carefully under his long cloak, he hurried back to his room. He hid the leg of gold in his closet. Then he went to bed and immediately fell into a deep sleep.

The following morning, the gravekeeper was working in the churchyard. As he neared the lady's grave, he heard a voice calling, "Gold, gold, give me back my leg of gold!" All morning the voice kept calling. Finally the gravekeeper hurried to the lord and said, "Sir, your wife is calling from the grave. I cannot do my work. You must go and see what it is that she wants."

The lord rushed down to his wife's grave and said, "My darling wife, what is it that you wish to tell me?"

"Gold, gold, give me back my leg of gold!" came the reply.

"But my dear," the lord replied, "you already have your leg of gold. Is there nothing you wish to say to me?"

But the voice only repeated, "Gold, gold, give me back my leg of gold!"

"Well, if that is all you can say, I wish you good day! I will remember you in my prayers!" And he marched back to the manor.

But the voice did not stop calling all that morning. The gravedigger was distraught. He went to the lord once again. "My lord. Your wife will not rest. Please send someone to her," he pleaded.

So the lord sent the lady's maid out to the churchyard.

"What can I do for you, m'lady?" the maid asked.

"Gold, gold, give me back my leg of gold!" was the reply.

"But m'lady. Be reasonable! You already have your leg of gold!"

"Gold, gold, give me back my leg of gold!" said the voice again.

"M'lady," said the maid, "You are not being fair. I cannot give you what you already have. I will pray for you this evening. Good day." And the maid returned to the manor.

The voice continued to call.

"Gold, gold, give me back my leg of gold!"

The gravekeeper returned to the lord.

"My lord, your wife keeps calling. Please, you must send someone to her," he pleaded again.

The lord turned to his groom. "Go and see if you can figure out what it is she wants," he said.

"My lord, I cannot," the groom replied, his lips quivering.

"What? Will you disobey your master? Go immediately!" the lord shouted.

"Please, my lord, do not ask me again. I cannot go!" the groom pleaded, tears running down his face.

"You coward! Go at once or you will be dead by morning!" the lord replied angrily.

The groom turned and walked to the churchyard, his heart knocking painfully against his ribs.

When he reached his lady's grave, he whispered, "M'lady, what is it that you want?"

"It is *you* that I want!" screamed the lady.

Suddenly a long, white ghost rose from the ground and grabbed the groom by the throat. The lady dragged him under the ground with her and ate him up, *beginning with his leg.*

Ah, Are You Digging on My Grave?

THOMAS HARDY

"Ah, are you digging on my grave,
　　My loved one? — planting rue?"
— "No: yesterday he went to wed
One of the brightest wealth has bred.
'It cannot hurt her now', he said,
　　'That I should not be true'."

"Then who is digging on my grave,
　　My nearest dearest kin?"
— "Ah, no: they sit and think, 'What use!
What good will planting flowers produce?
No tendance of her mound can loose
　　Her spirit from Death's gin'."

"But someone digs upon my grave?
My enemy? — prodding sly?"
— "Nay: when she heard you had passed the Gate
That shuts on all flesh soon or late,
She thought you no more worth her hate,
And cares not where you lie."

"Then, who is digging on my grave?
Say — since I have not guessed!"
— "O it is I, my mistress dear,
Your little dog, who still lives near,
And much I hope my movements here
Have not disturbed your rest?"

"Ah yes! You dig upon my grave . . .
Why flashed it not to me
That one true heart was left behind!
What feeling do we ever find
To equal among human kind
A dog's fidelity!"

"Mistress, I dug upon your grave
To bury a bone, in case
I should be hungry near this spot
When passing on my daily trot.
I am sorry, but I quite forgot
It was your resting place."

Frankenstein

MARY SHELLEY

(excerpt)

It was on a dreary night of November that I beheld the accomplishment of my toils. With an anxiety that almost amounted to agony, I collected the instruments of life around me, that I might infuse a spark of being into the lifeless thing that lay at my feet. It was already one in the morning; the rain pattered dismally against the panes, and my candle was nearly burnt out, when, by the glimmer of the half-extinguished light, I saw the dull yellow eye of the creature open; it breathed hard, and a convulsive motion agitated its limbs.

How can I describe my emotions at this catastrophe, or how delineate the wretch whom with such infinite pains and care I had endeavored to form? His limbs were in proportion, and I had selected his features as beautiful. Beautiful! Great God! His yellow skin scarcely covered the work of muscles and arteries beneath; his hair was of a lustrous black, and flowing; his teeth of a pearly whiteness; but these luxuriances only formed a more horrid contrast with his watery eyes, that seemed almost of the same color as the dun-white sockets in which they were set, his shriveled complexion and straight black lips.

The different accidents of life are not so changeable as the feelings of human nature. I had worked hard for nearly two years, for the sole purpose of infusing life into an inanimate body. For this I had deprived myself of rest and health. I had desired it with an ardor that far exceeded moderation; but now that I had finished, the beauty of the dream vanished, and breathless horror and disgust filled my heart. Unable to endure the aspect of the being I had created, I rushed out of the room and continued a long time traversing my bed-chamber, unable to compose my mind to sleep. At length lassitude succeeded to the tumult I had before endured, and I threw myself on the bed in my clothes, endeavoring to seek a few moments of forgetfulness. But it was in vain; I slept, indeed, but I was disturbed by the wildest dreams. I thought I saw Elizabeth, in the bloom of health, walking in the streets of Ingolstadt. Delighted and surprised, I embraced her, but as I imprinted the first kiss on her lips, they became livid with the hue of death; her features appeared to change, and I thought that I held the corpse of my dead mother in my arms; a shroud enveloped her form, and I saw the grave-worms crawling in the folds of the flannel. I started from my sleep with horror; a cold dew covered my forehead, my teeth chattered, and every limb became convulsed; when, by the dim and yellow light of the moon, as it forced its way through the window shutters, I beheld the wretch — the miserable monster whom I had created. He held up the curtain of the bed; and his eyes, if eyes they may be called, were fixed on me. His jaws opened, and he muttered some inarticulate sounds, while a grin wrinkled his cheeks. He might have spoken, but I did not hear; one hand was stretched out, seemingly to detain me, but I escaped and rushed downstairs. I took refuge in the courtyard belonging to the house which I inhabited, where I remained during the rest of the night, walking up and down in the greatest agitation, listening attentively, catching and fearing each sound as if it were to announce the approach of the demoniacal corpse to which I had so miserably given life.

Oh! No mortal could support the horror of that countenance. A mummy again endued with animation could not be so hideous as that wretch. I had gazed on him while unfinished; he was ugly then, but when those muscles and joints were rendered capable of motion, it became a thing such as even Dante could not have conceived.

I passed the night wretchedly. Sometimes my pulse beat so quickly and hardly that I felt the palpitation of every artery; at others, I nearly sank to the ground through languor and extreme weakness. Mingled with this horror, I felt the bitterness of disappointment; dreams that had been my food and pleasant rest for so long a space were now become a hell to me; and the change was so rapid, the overthrow so complete!

Morning, dismal and wet, at length dawned and discovered to my sleepless and aching eyes the church of Ingolstadt, its white steeple and clock, which indicated the sixth hour. The porter opened the gates of the court, which had that night been my asylum, and I issued into the streets, pacing them with quick steps, as if I sought to avoid the wretch whom I feared every turning of the street would present to my view. I did not dare return to the apartment which I inhabited, but felt impelled to hurry on, although drenched by the rain which poured from a black and comfortless sky.

The Honest Ghost

SORCHE NIC LEODHAS

When the old Laird of Thistleton died it caused very little stir in the neighborhood. The estate was large and there were many tenants on it: farmers, crofters, shepherds on the various properties; a miller who tended a mill beside a busy stream; and numerous villagers, for the village of Balnacairn lay within the estate. But the Laird was an old man and had lived out his time. Although respected, he was not regretted much. No one was greatly concerned about his passing or troubled about the future. The old Laird was dead, God rest his soul, and now there would be a new laird to take over. It was expected things would be going on in the way they had always done before.

He died quite suddenly, but quietly, in his sleep on a cold and frosty October night, having just come home shortly before from a visit to the minister at Balnacairn village six miles away. For an old man he was unusually vigorous and had made the journey to the village and back that night on foot.

He was laid to rest in the churchyard, and those who had come to his funeral to pay their respects, if not to mourn, turned away and left him lying there among those of his family who for generations had been buried there.

Folk thereabout agreed that there was little to be said against the old Laird. To be sure, he was crabbed and cross-grained, and easily provoked into a rage. But as a master, he was just and fair-minded. And he was honest. Such a man, one could be certain, would rest peacefully in his grave.

The first word of it came on a cold damp evening about six weeks or so after the old Laird's funeral. The folk of Balnacairn village, alarmed at hearing the sounds of horses' hoofs pounding and the rumble of the wheels of a heavy cart coming down the road that led into the town, ran to their doors to find out what could be the matter.

Presently, two horses and the wagon they hauled loomed out of the misty drizzle and stopped before the inn. The villagers crowded about the wagon and found the driver, Lang Tammas the carter, lying against the wooden back of the seat, and shaking like a man in a fit. He stared at them with wide-open eyes, and his face was as white as sifted flour. It was a while before they could get any words out of him that made sense. Something had certainly given the man a terrible shock. They helped him down from the cart and took him into the inn, where the innkeeper brought him a wee glass of brandy to soothe his nerves, and after a while he began to come to himself again. But when he could talk what he said didn't have much sense in it at all.

Lang Tammas had gone over to the mill, which stood a few miles beyond Thistleton Manor, to take some sacks of corn to be ground for the minister of Balnacairn. It was when he was coming back that he got the terrible fright. As he came up to the gates of Thistleton Manor he saw a man standing in the middle of the drive between the stone gateposts. The mist was rising heavier there because of the burn that ran along beside the road, so he couldn't see the man distinctly at first, but he looked familiar to Lang Tammas. It wasn't until the carter drove right up close that he got a good look at the man. It was then that Tammas saw that it was the Laird of Thistleton himself!

"The old Laird, it was, and he stepping out toward the cart, I'm telling you," said Tammas. "He had a big brass lantern in his hand. It was not lit, and he held it up and shook it at me. Then he called me by name, he did. 'Look ye here, Lang Tammas!' said he, and made to come closer, but I was in no mind to wait to hear what he would say. I whipped up the horses and hastened away at a gallop, and left him by the gate there!"

Well, that was the tale Lang Tammas told, and there were some who believed him but there were more who did not, and the latter said that Lang Tammas had a wee bit too much to drink with the miller, while waiting for the minister's corn to be ground.

No doubt the matter would have been forgotten after a while if nothing else had happened, but a month later the old Laird appeared again, and not in the dusk of a misty evening but in the clear light of day.

It was Jamie the Post who got sight of the Laird this time, while Jamie was bringing the post-bags from the railway station at Balquidder to the postmistress at Balnacairn. Jamie was ambling along in the post cart at an easy pace, it not being his way to hurry himself at any time. When he was passing the gates of Thistleton Manor he gave a careless glance up the drive and there in the doorway of the gatehouse, just inside the manor gates, he saw the old Laird of Thistleton standing, with the big brass lantern in his hand. The Laird waved the lantern at Jamie, but Jamie did not wait to see if the Laird would come nearer, or to hear if he called Jamie by name. Jamie whipped up the pony that drew the post

cart, and they dashed madly down the road and into the village of Balnacairn, and folk there said his speed was an achievement that Jamie never equaled before or after.

No one could blame what Jamie saw on his having had a drink or two too many, for it was well known that Jamie was a strong temperance man and had never in his life taken a drink. Maybe there was something in it after all, folk told each other. Nobody cared to talk much about it, now that the Laird had been seen twice. Such things don't bear talking about that happen so close to home. But nobody, if he could help it, went anywhere near Thistleton Manor after the day the old Laird was seen for the second time.

Well, the old Laird's estate was settled at last, and as he had neither wife nor bairns of his own, he left all he had to his nephew, the only son of a brother who had gone to Australia and settled there. The title went to the nephew, too, so now there was a new Laird of Thistleton, as well as the old Laird, who seemed to be still lingering about the place.

Folk began to wonder how the old Laird would get along when the new Laird came to take over the estate.

The new Laird did not come home to Thistleton Manor at once. He had established a business where he lived and needed time to dispose of it profitably. Besides, the sea journey was long and the time of year was not the best for traveling. The new Laird and his wife had a very young child and thought they'd rather wait until the child was older and the conditions of weather better before making so long a journey with him. So the estate was put into the hands of an estate agent in Edinburgh, who was to see to the managing of the lands and the farms and the tenants, until the new Laird came home. As for the manor house itself, the agent was to find a tenant for it, with a short lease of no more than a year, if he could.

The agent had no trouble in finding a tenant. It was a desirable property, as the notice in the papers said, and the house was nicely furnished and well kept up. The agent found not only one tenant, but three. One after another they came and left, all driven out, one after another, because they could not bear the sight of the old Laird with the big brass lantern in his hand.

After the third tenant left, in a high state of indignation, there were no more tenants, because by that time the word had gone around that the place was haunted, and as the estate agent said, "Who in the world would ever want to rent a haunted house?"

That was the way matter stood when the new Laird of Thistleton finally came over the seas to take up his estates. He did not go immediately to Thistleton Manor, but stopped in Edinburgh to talk to the agent whom he had put in charge of his affairs.

He settled his wife and child at a comfortable hotel and went to the office of the agent. He had never been in Scotland before and knew very little about his inheritance. He found the agent in his office, and the minute he laid eyes on the man, the new Laird knew that something was amiss. He knew, too, that the agent did not want to tell him what it was. The new Laird could not lay his finger on the trouble. The agent seemed ready enough to talk about the estate. He brought out a map with the lands marked upon it: the mill, the farms, the church, the village, the manor and all in their places, with the names of the tenants beside them. He brought out other accounts and they were all in order. No trouble about anything there, as the new Laird could see for himself. Yet the agent seemed to be uneasy about something. What on earth could it be?

The new Laird picked up the accounts and looked at them again, and something caught his eye that he had not noticed before.

"I'm a plain man, and I'll ask you a plain question," he told the agent. "What is wrong with the manor house?"

"Nothing at all!" the agent answered quickly. Too quickly, the new Laird said to himself.

"The house is in fine shape. Well-cared for, and nicely furnished. You could not ask for a better-kept house."

"If that is so," the new Laird said. "Why is it that in the first six months after my uncle's death three tenants, one after another, signed up for the house, expecting to stay for a year, and every one of them cleared out before the end of the month? And since the last one left, no one has taken the manor house at all? What is wrong with the place?"

"Well," said the agent reluctantly. "They say it's haunted!"

The new Laird of Thistleton looked at the agent in disbelief. "Haunted!" he exclaimed. "It could not be. My father loved the place and never tired of talking of it. He'd have taken delight in an old family ghost, and I'm sure we'd have heard about it if there had been one there."

"It is not an old family ghost that was seen," the agent said. "At any rate, not a *very* old ghost. In fact, it is the ghost of your late uncle, as I understand. They say he carries a great brass lantern and shakes it in their faces. Most alarming, I am sure."

The new Laird looked at the agent in silence for a while. Then he got up to take his leave. "I'll look into it," he promised, and went his way.

The new Laird of Thistleton went back to his hotel and told his wife what the agent had said.

"My goodness!" said she, "Poor Uncle Andrew! He must find it very uncomfortable to be a ghost. I wonder what makes him do it?"

"So do I," said the new Laird. "And what's more, I mean to find out."

They decided to go, not to Thistleton Manor, but to the village of Balnacairn.

The village was only six miles from the manor, which was no distance at all, and the agent had said there was a very good inn where they would be able to stay. They felt that the inn would be the best place to carry on their investigations from, and besides, the new Laird's wife was not sure it would be a good thing for the

baby if they went to stay at Thistleton Manor and Uncle Andrew were to appear and shake his big brass lantern at them.

Fortunately, they were able to find lodging at the inn, and the landlady was pleased when she learned that it was the new Laird and his family who were sheltering under her roof. Perhaps it was the pleasure that the honor thus paid gave her that loosened her tongue. At any rate, before a day had passed, she had told the new Laird and his wife all about the way the old Laird's ghost had appeared to Lang Tammas the carter and to Jamie the Post, and as the tenants had fled to the inn from Thistleton Manor, she could tell about their experiences, too.

The new Laird and his wife were pleasant folk and friendly, and not the sort to set themselves up above others, as folk said, so the tenantry accepted them at once. It wasn't that they had anything against the old Laird, you understand, but they could see that this new man would make a very good laird. So nobody minded at all answering any questions the new Laird and his lady asked.

What the new Laird and his wife wanted to find out was, what kept the old Laird from resting quietly in his grave? What sort of man had he been when he was alive?

Well, folk said, he was a crabbed old creature, so he was, but he was just.

He worked his men hard, but then he was a hard worker himself. And he was honest. He always gave an honest day's pay for an honest day's work. He had a terrible temper and would fly into a sudden rage if anyone crossed him, but to tell the truth, he never was angry without a good reason. He couldn't abide dishonesty, being an honest man himself. He could stretch a penny farther than any other man, but a man could count on getting what was due him, although probably he'd get no more. He was an honest man, the old Laird was.

The minister, who had been the old man's only close friend, smiled when he was asked what the old Laird was like. "Not so bad as he liked to make out," he said. "He was a bit crusty and short-tempered at times, but he was more honest than any other man I know. It would have been as impossible for the Laird to lie, or cheat, or steal, as for him to pick up a mountain and hold it in one hand."

Everybody did feel sorry for the new Laird and his lady, with them coming such a long distance only to find that the manor house was not habitable on account of the ghost. They would have helped gladly, but though they racked their brains, they could not say what was troubling the old Laird so that he could not rest in his grave.

The new Laird and his wife put their heads together and compared notes on everything they had been told.

"The old Laird was a terrible old curmudgeon," said the new Laird.

"But he was honest," said his wife.

"He was a penny pincher," said the new Laird.

"But he was honest," said his wife.

"He had a way, at times, of flying into a terrible rage," said the new Laird.

"But he was honest," said the Laird's wife. "No matter what anyone said about him, every single one of them said that he was honest. I don't think that a man as honest as your Uncle Andrew would be haunting Thistleton Manor just to keep you away. Not after he'd left it to you in his will!"

"I think you are right!" her husband said. "There's no doubt about his honesty. Everybody speaks of it."

His wife said nothing for a while, then she said slowly, "There is something else about your uncle that everybody mentions. When they speak about his ghost, I mean. The tenants told the agent, Lang Tammas the carter and Jamie the Post told the folk here at Balnacairn. When anyone ever says anything about the ghost they say 'and he shook his big brass lantern in his face!' *Everyone* says it."

They looked at each other for minute in silence. Then, "Tomorrow," said the new Laird, "we will go to Thistleton Manor."

"And see if there is a big brass lantern there," said his wife.

So the next day they left the baby with the landlady at the inn and borrowed a pony and cart from the landlord, and off they went.

They went up the drive and got out of the cart, and the young Laird opened the door with the key the agent had given him. They went into the house and searched from room to room, upstairs and down. Not a sign of a big brass lantern did they see, nor of the old Laird's ghost, for that matter.

"Uncle Andrew's lantern must be the ghost of a lantern," the new Laird said, as they came down to the hall again.

His wife had gone to the other end of the passage and was standing before a door. "What door is this?" she asked, trying the knob. "It's locked. Where does it lead to?"

"Probably into the garden," said the new Laird.

"I don't think it does," said his wife. "The rooms on either side go back farther. I think it's a room, a small one."

"Of course it is!" the new Laird said. "I know what it is. It's my uncle's estate office. The agent told me about it. He locked it up when he took charge of the estate because there were private papers here and he wanted them to be kept safe. Wait a minute! I think he gave me the key."

The key was found and the door was opened. The first thing they saw was the big brass lantern standing on the shelf above the old Laird's desk.

The new Laird's wife took down the lantern. "Look," she said. There was a tag tied by a string to the ring at the top. They saw there were words written carefully on the tag. "The minister's lantern. Balnacairn," they read. They looked at each other.

"Poor Uncle Andrew!" the new Laird's wife said. "All he wanted was for someone to take the lantern back to its rightful owner. It didn't belong to him, and he couldn't rest in his grave knowing it hadn't been returned."

They took the lantern back to the minister that very day. He

took it in his hand. "Why, I'd forgotten he had it," the minister said. "I remember now. He borrowed it the last time he was here, before he died. He had stayed late, for we got to talking and never noticed the time, and it was dark when he started out for home. So I let him take the lantern to light him home."

The next day the Laird and his wife and his child packed up and moved into Thistleton Manor. They were quite sure the old Laird's ghost was at rest, now that the lantern was back where it belonged. And they were right.

Folk kept a close watch for a while, but everything at the manor seemed to be going on very well, and as far as anybody

could tell the ghost was gone for good. So Lang Tammas the carter began to haul his corn to the mill, and Jamie the Post to carry the post-bags along the road past Thistleton Manor again, instead of taking the longer road the way they'd been going since they met the old Laird's ghost.

The new Laird and his wife called their second son Andrew after the old Laird, and he was very like him in temperament, for he was given to spells of being crabbed and crusty, often flying into a rage. But his mother said she did not mind, as long as he grew up to be as honest as the old Laird, because the old Laird, as everyone always said, was a very honest man.

Annabel Lee

EDGAR ALLAN POE

It was many and many a year ago,
In a kingdom by the sea,
That a maiden there lived whom you may know
By the name of Annabel Lee.
And this maiden she lived with no other thought
Than to love and be loved by me.

I was a child and she was a child
In this kingdom by the sea:
But we loved with a love that was more than love —
I and my Annabel Lee,
With a love that the wingèd seraphs of heaven
Coveted her and me.

And this was the reason that, long ago,
In this kingdom by the sea,
A wind blew out of a cloud, chilling
My beautiful Annabel Lee,

So that her high-born kinsmen came
And bore her away from me,
To shut her up in a sepulchre
In this kingdom by the sea.

The angels, not half so happy in heaven,
Went envying her and me —
Yes! That was the reason (as all men know,
In this kingdom by the sea)
That the wind came out of the cloud one night,
Chilling and killing my Annabel Lee.

But our love it was stronger by far than the love
Of those who were older than we —
Of many far wiser than we —
And neither the angels in heaven above,
Nor the demons down under the sea,
Can ever dissever my soul from the soul
Of the beautiful Annabel Lee:

For the moon never beams without bringing me dreams
Of the beautiful Annabel Lee;
And the stars never rise, but I feel the bright eyes
Of the beautiful Annabel Lee;
And so, all the night-tide, I lie down by the side
Of my darling — my darling — my life and my bride,
In the sepulchre there by the sea,
In her tomb by the sounding sea.

The Gorgon's Head

NATHANIEL HAWTHORNE

Perseus was the son of Danaë, who was the daughter of a king. And when Perseus was a very little boy, some wicked people put his mother and himself into a chest, and set them afloat upon the sea. The wind blew freshly, and drove the chest away from the shore, and the uneasy billows, tossed it up and down; while Danaë clasped her child closely to her bosom, and dreaded that some big wave would dash its foamy crest over them both. The chest sailed on, however, and neither sank nor was upset; until, when night was coming, it floated so near an island that it got entangled in a fisherman's nets, and was drawn out high and dry upon the sand. The island was called Seriphus, and it was reigned over by King Polydectes, who happened to be the fisherman's brother.

This fisherman, I am glad to tell you, was an exceedingly humane and upright man. He showed great kindness to Danaë and her little boy; and continued to befriend them, until Perseus had grown to be a handsome youth, very strong and active, and skillful in the use of arms. Long before this time, King Polydectes had seen the two strangers — the mother and her child — who had come to his dominions in a floating chest. As he was not good and kind, like his brother the fisherman, but extremely wicked, he resolved to send Perseus on a dangerous enterprise, in which he would probably be killed, and then to do some great mischief to Danaë herself. So this bad-hearted king spent a long while in considering what was the most dangerous thing that a young man could possibly undertake to perform. At last, having hit upon an enterprise that promised to turn out as fatally as he desired, he sent for the youthful Perseus.

The young man came to the palace, and found the king sitting upon his throne.

"Perseus," said King Polydectes, smiling craftily upon him, "you are grown up a fine young man. You and your good mother have received a great deal of kindness from myself, as well as from my worthy brother the fisherman, and I suppose you would not be sorry to repay some of it."

"Please your Majesty," answered Perseus, "I would willingly risk my life to do so."

"Well, then," continued the king, still with a cunning smile on his lips, "I have a little adventure to propose to you; and, as you are a brave and enterprising youth, you will doubtless look upon it as a great piece of good luck to have so rare an opportunity of distinguishing yourself. You must know, my good Perseus, I think of getting married to the beautiful Princess Hippodamia; and it is customary, on these occasions, to make the bride a present of some farfetched and elegant curiosity. I have been a little perplexed, I must honestly confess, where to obtain anything likely to please a princess of her exquisite taste. But, this morning, I flatter myself, I have thought of precisely the article."

"And can I assist your Majesty in obtaining it?" cried Perseus, eagerly.

"You can, if you are as brave a youth as I believe you to be," replied King Polydectes, with the utmost graciousness of manner.

"The bridal gift which I have set my heart on presenting to the beautiful Hippodamia is the head of the Gorgon Medusa with the snaky locks; and I depend on you, my dear Perseus, to bring it to me. So, as I am anxious to settle affairs with the princess, the sooner you go in quest of the Gorgon, the better I shall be pleased."

"I will set out tomorrow morning," answered Perseus.

"Pray do so, my gallant youth," rejoined the king. "And, Perseus, in cutting off the Gorgon's head, be careful to make a clean stroke, so as not to injure its appearance. You must bring it home in the very best condition, in order to suit the exquisite taste of the beautiful Princess Hippodamia."

Perseus left the palace, but was scarcely out of hearing before Polydectes burst into a laugh; being greatly amused, wicked king that he was, to find how readily the young man fell into the snare. The news quickly spread abroad that Perseus had undertaken to cut off the head of Medusa with the snaky locks. Everybody was rejoiced; for most of the inhabitants of the island were as wicked as the king himself, and would have liked nothing better than to see some enormous mischief happen to Danaë and her son. The only good man in this unfortunate island of Seriphus appears to have been the fisherman. As Perseus walked along, therefore, the people pointed after him, and made mouths, and winked to one another, and ridiculed him as loudly as they dared.

"Ho, ho!" cried they; "Medusa's snakes will sting him soundly!"

Now, there were three Gorgons alive at that period; and they were the most strange and terrible monsters that had ever been since the world was made, or that have been seen in after days, or that are likely to be seen in all time to come. I hardly know what sort of creature or hobgoblin to call them. They were three sisters, and seem to have borne some distant resemblance to women, but were really a very frightful and mischievous species of dragon. It

is, indeed, difficult to imagine what hideous beings these three sisters were. Why, instead of locks of hair, if you can believe me, they had each of them a hundred enormous snakes growing on their heads, all alive, twisting, wriggling, curling, and thrusting out their venomous tongues, with forked stings at the end! The teeth of the Gorgons were terribly long tusks; their hands were made of brass; and their bodies were all over scales, which, if not iron, were something as hard and impenetrable. They had wings, too, and exceedingly splendid ones, I can assure you; for every feather in them was pure, bright, glittering, burnished gold, and they looked very dazzlingly, no doubt, when the Gorgons were flying about in the sunshine.

But when people happened to catch a glimpse of their glittering brightness, aloft in the air, they seldom stopped to gaze, but ran and hid themselves as speedily as they could. You will think, perhaps, that they were afraid of being stung by the serpents that served the Gorgons instead of hair — or of having their heads bitten off by their ugly tusks — or of being torn all to pieces by their brazen claws. Well, to be sure, these were some of the dangers, but by no means the greatest, nor the most difficult to avoid. For the worst thing about these abominable Gorgons was, that, if once a poor mortal fixed his eyes full upon one of their faces, he was certain, that very instant to be changed from warm flesh and blood into cold and lifeless stone!

Thus, as you will easily perceive, it was a very dangerous adventure that the wicked King Polydectes had contrived for this innocent young man. Perseus himself, when he had thought over the matter, could not help seeing that he had very little chance of coming safely through it, and that he was far more likely to become a stone image than to bring back the head of Medusa with the snaky locks. For, not to speak of other difficulties, there was one which it would have puzzled an older man than Perseus to get over. Not only must he fight with and slay this golden-winged, iron-scaled, long-tusked, brazen-clawed, snaky-haired monster, but he must do it with his eyes shut, or, at least, without so much as a glance at the enemy with whom he was contending. Else, while his arm was lifted to strike, he would stiffen into stone, and stand with that uplifted arm for centuries, until time, and the wind and weather, should crumble him quite away. This would be a very sad thing to befall a young man who wanted to perform a great many brave deeds, and to enjoy a great deal of happiness, in this bright and beautiful world.

So disconsolate did these thoughts make him, that Perseus could not bear to tell his mother what he had undertaken to do.

He therefore took his shield, girded on his sword, and crossed over from the island to the mainland, where he sat down in a solitary place, and hardly refrained from shedding tears.

But, while he was in this sorrowful mood, he heard a voice close beside him.

"Perseus," said the voice, "why are you sad?"

He lifted his head from his hands, in which he had hidden it, and, behold! all alone as Perseus had supposed himself to be, there was a stranger in the solitary place. It was a brisk, intelligent, and remarkably shrewd-looking young man, with a cloak over his shoulders, an odd sort of cap on his head, a strangely twisted staff in his hand, and a short and very crooked sword hanging by his side. He was exceedingly light and active in his figure, like a person much accustomed to gymnastic exercises, and well able to leap or run. Above all, the stranger had such a cheerful, knowing, and helpful aspect (though it was certainly a little mischievous, into the bargain), that Perseus could not help feeling his spirits grow livelier as he gazed at him. Besides, being really a courageous youth, he felt greatly ashamed that anybody should have found him with tears in his eyes, like a timid little schoolboy, when, after all, there might be no occasion for despair. So Perseus wiped his eyes, and answered the stranger pretty briskly, putting on as brave a look as he could.

"I am not so very sad," said he, "only thoughtful about an adventure that I have undertaken."

"Oho!" answered the stranger. "Well, tell me all about it, and possibly I may be of service to you. I have helped a good many young men through adventures that looked difficult enough beforehand. Perhaps you may have heard of me. I have more names than one; but the name of Quicksilver suits me as well as any other. Tell me what the trouble is, and we will talk the matter over, and see what can be done."

The stranger's words and manner put Perseus into quite a different mood from his former one. He resolved to tell Quicksilver all his difficulties, since he could not easily be worse off than he already was, and, very possibly, his new friend might give him some advice that would turn out well in the end. So he let the stranger know, in few words, precisely what the case was — how that King Polydectes wanted the head of Medusa with the snaky locks as a bridal gift for the beautiful Princess Hippodamia, and how that he had undertaken to get it for him, but was afraid of being turned into stone.

"And that would be a great pity," said Quicksilver, with his mischievous smile. "You would make a very handsome marble statue, it is true, and it would be a considerable number of centuries before you crumbled away; but, on the whole, one would rather be a young man for a few years, than a stone image for a great many."

"Oh, far rather!" exclaimed Perseus, with the tears again standing in his eyes. "And, besides, what would my dear mother do, if her beloved son were turned into a stone?"

"Well, well, let us hope that the affair will not turn out so very badly," replied Quicksilver, in an encouraging tone. "I am the very person to help you, if anybody can. My sister and myself will do our utmost to bring you safe though the adventure, ugly as it now looks."

"Your sister?" repeated Perseus.

"Yes, my sister," said the stranger. "She is very wise, I promise you; and as for myself, I generally have all my wits about me, such as they are. If you show yourself bold and cautious, and follow our advice, you need not fear being a stone image yet awhile. But, first of all, you must polish your shield, till you can see your face in it as distinctly as in a mirror."

This seemed to Perseus rather an odd beginning of the adventure; for he thought it of far more consequence that the shield should be strong enough to defend him from the Gorgon's brazen claws, than that it should be bright enough to show him the reflection of his face. However, concluding that Quicksilver knew better than himself, he immediately set to work, and scrubbed the shield with so much diligence and goodwill, that it very quickly shone like the moon at harvesttime. Quicksilver looked at it with a smile, and nodded his approbation. Then, taking off his own short and crooked sword, he girded it about Perseus, instead of the one which he had before worn.

"No sword but mine will answer your purpose," observed he; "the blade has a most excellent temper, and will cut through iron

and brass as easily as through the slenderest twig. And now we will set out. The next thing is to find the Three Gray Women, who will tell us where to find the Nymphs."

"The Three Gray Women!" cried Perseus, to whom this seemed only a new difficulty in the path of his adventure; "pray who may the Three Gray Women be? I never heard of them before."

"They are three very strange old ladies," said Quicksilver, laughing. "They have but one eye among them, and only one tooth. Moreover, you must find them out by starlight, or in the dusk of the evening; for they never show themselves by the light either of the sun or moon."

"But," said Perseus, "why should I waste my time with these Three Gray Women? Would it not be better to set out at once in search of the terrible Gorgons?"

"No, no," answered his friend. "There are other things to be done, before you can find your way to the Gorgons. There is nothing for it but to hunt up these old ladies; and when we meet with them, you may be sure that the Gorgons are not a great way off. Come, let us be stirring!"

Perseus, by this time, felt so much confidence in his companion's sagacity, that he made no more objections, and professed himself ready to begin the adventure immediately. They accordingly set out, and walked at a pretty brisk pace; so brisk, indeed, that Perseus found it rather difficult to keep up with his nimble friend Quicksilver. To say the truth, he had a singular idea that Quicksilver was furnished with a pair of winged shoes, which, of course, helped him along marvelously. And then, too, when Perseus looked sideways at him, out of the corner of his eye, he seemed to see wings on the side of his head; although, if he turned a full gaze, there were no such things to be perceived, but only an odd kind of cap. But, at all events, the twisted staff was evidently a great convenience to Quicksilver, and enabled him to proceed so fast, that Perseus, though a remarkably active young man, began to be out of breath.

"Here!" cried Quicksilver, at last — for he knew well enough, rogue that he was, how hard Perseus found it to keep pace with him — "take you the staff, for you need it a great deal more than I. Are there no better walkers than yourself in the island of Seriphus?"

"I could walk pretty well," said Perseus, glancing slyly at his companion's feet, "if I had only a pair of winged shoes."

"We must see about getting you a pair," answered Quicksilver.

But the staff helped Perseus along so bravely, that he no longer felt the slightest weariness. In fact, the stick seemed to be alive in his hand, and to lend some of its life to Perseus. He and Quicksilver now walked onward at their ease, talking very sociably together; and Quicksilver told so many pleasant stories about his former adventures, and how well his wits had served him on various occasions, that Perseus began to think him a very wonderful person. He evidently knew the world; and nobody is so charming to a young man as a friend who has that kind of knowledge. Perseus listened the more eagerly, in the hope of brightening his own wits by what he heard.

At last, he happened to recollect that Quicksilver had spoken of a sister, who was to lend her assistance in the adventure which they were now bound upon.

"Where is she?" he inquired. "Shall we not meet her soon?"

"All at the proper time," said his companion. "But this sister of mine, you must understand, is quite a different sort of character from myself. She is very grave and prudent, seldom smiles, never laughs, and makes it a rule not to utter a word unless she has something particularly profound to say. Neither will she listen to any but the wisest conversation."

"Dear me!" ejaculated Perseus; "I shall be afraid to say a syllable."

"She is a very accomplished person, I assure you," continued Quicksilver, "and has all the arts and sciences at her fingers' ends. In short, she is so immoderately wise, that many people call her wisdom personified. But, to tell you the truth, she has hardly vivacity enough for my taste; and I think you would scarcely find her so pleasant a traveling companion as myself. She has her good points, nevertheless; and you will find the benefit of them, in your encounter with the Gorgons."

By this time it had grown quite dusk. They were now come to a very wild and desert place, overgrown with shaggy bushes, and so silent and solitary that nobody seemed ever to have dwelt or journeyed there. All was waste and desolate, in the gray twilight, which grew every moment more obscure. Perseus looked about him, rather disconsolately, and asked Quicksilver whether they had a great deal farther to go.

"Hist! hist!" whispered his companion. "Make no noise! This is just the time and place to meet the Three Gray Women. Be careful that they do not see you before you see them; for, though they have but a single eye among the three, it is as sharp-sighted as half a dozen common eyes."

"But what must I do," asked Perseus, "when we meet them?"

Quicksilver explained to Perseus how the Three Gray Women managed with their one eye. They were in the habit, it seems, of changing it from one to another, as if it had been a pair of spectacles, or — which would have suited them better — a quizzing-glass. When one of the three had kept the eye a certain time, she took it out of the socket and passed it to one of her sisters, whose turn it might happen to be, and who immediately clapped it into her own head, and enjoyed a peep at the visible world. Thus it will easily be understood that only one of the Three Gray Women could see, while the other two were in utter darkness; and, moreover, at the instant when the eye was passing from hand to hand, neither of the poor old ladies was able to see a wink. I have heard of a great many strange things, in my day, and have witnessed not a few; but none, it seems to me, that can compare with the oddity of these Three Gray Women, all peeping through a single eye.

So thought Perseus, likewise, and was so astonished that he almost fancied his companion was joking with him, and that there were no such old women in the world.

"You will soon find whether I tell the truth or no," observed

Quicksilver. "Hark! hush! hist! hist! There they come, now!"

Perseus looked earnestly through the dusk of the evening, and there, sure enough, at no great distance off, he descried the Three Gray Women. The light being so faint, he could not well make out what sort of figures they were; only he discovered that they had long gray hair; and, as they came nearer, he saw that two of them had but the empty socket of an eye, in the middle of their foreheads. But, in the middle of the third sister's forehead, there was a very large, bright, and piercing eye, which sparkled like a great diamond in a ring; and so penetrating did it seem to be, that Perseus could not help thinking it must possess the gift of seeing in the darkest midnight just as perfectly as at noonday. The sight of three persons' eyes was melted and collected into that single one.

Thus the three old dames got along about as comfortably, upon the whole, as if they could all see at once. She who chanced to have the eye in her forehead led the other two by the hands, peeping sharply about her, all the while; insomuch that Perseus dreaded lest she should see right through the thick clump of bushes behind which he and Quicksilver had hidden themselves. My stars! it was positively terrible to be within reach of so very sharp an eye!

But, before they reached the clump of bushes, one of the Three Gray Women spoke.

"Sister! Sister Scarecrow!" cried she, "you have had the eye long enough. It is my turn now!"

"Let me keep it a moment longer, Sister Nightmare," answered Scarecrow. "I thought I had a glimpse of something behind that thick bush."

"Well, and what of that?" retorted Nightmare, peevishly. "Can't I see into a thick bush as easily as yourself? The eye is mine as well as yours; and I know the use of it as well as you, or may be a little better. I insist upon taking a peep immediately!"

But here the third sister, whose name was Shakejoint, began to complain, and said that it was her turn to have the eye, and that Scarecrow and Nightmare wanted to keep it all to themselves. To end the dispute, old Dame Scarecrow took the eye out of her forehead, and held it forth in her hand.

"Take it, one of you," cried she, "and quit this foolish quarreling. For my part, I shall be glad of a little thick darkness. Take it quickly, however, or I must clap it into my own head again!"

Accordingly, both Nightmare and Shakejoint put out their hands, groping eagerly to snatch the eye out of the hand of Scarecrow. But, being both alike blind, they could not easily find where Scarecrow's hand was; and Scarecrow, being now just as much in the dark as Shakejoint and Nightmare, could not at once meet either of their hands, in order to put the eye into it. Thus (as

you will see, with half an eye, my wise little auditors), these good old dames had fallen into a strange perplexity. For, though the eye shone and glistened like a star, as Scarecrow held it out, yet the Gray Women caught not the least glimpse of its light, and were all three in utter darkness, from too impatient a desire to see.

Quicksilver was so much tickled at beholding Shakejoint and Nightmare both groping for the eye, and each finding fault with Scarecrow and one another, that he could scarcely help laughing aloud.

"Now is your time!" he whispered to Perseus. "Quick, quick! before they can clap the eye into either of their heads. Rush out upon the old ladies, and snatch it from Scarecrow's hand!"

In an instant, while the Three Gray Women were still scolding each other, Perseus leaped from behind the clump of bushes, and made himself master of the prize. The marvelous eye, as he held it in his hand, shone very brightly, and seemed to look up into his face with a knowing air, and an expression as if it would have winked, had it been provided with a pair of eyelids for that purpose. But the Gray Women knew nothing of what had happened; and, each supposing that one of her sisters was in possession of the eye, they began their quarrel anew. At last, as Perseus did not wish to put these respectable dames to greater inconvenience than was really necessary, he thought it right to explain the matter.

"My good ladies," said he, "pray do not be angry with one another. If anybody is in fault, it is myself; for I have the honor to hold your very brilliant and excellent eye in my own hand!"

"You! you have our eye! And who are you?" screamed the Three Gray Women, all in a breath; for they were terribly frightened, of course, at hearing a strange voice, and discovering that their eyesight had got into the hands of they could not guess whom. "Oh, what shall we do, sisters? what shall we do? We are all in the dark! Give us our eye! Give us our one, precious, solitary eye! You have two of your own! Give us our eye!"

"Tell them," whispered Quicksilver to Perseus, "that they shall have back the eye as soon as they direct you where to find the Nymphs who have the flying slippers, the magic wallet, and the helmet of invisibility."

"My dear, good, admirable old ladies," said Perseus, addressing the Gray Women, "there is no occasion for putting yourselves into such a fright. I am by no means a bad young man. You shall have back your eye, safe and sound, and as bright as ever, the moment you tell me where to find the Nymphs."

"The Nymphs! Goodness me! Sisters, what Nymphs does he mean?" screamed Scarecrow. "There are a great many Nymphs, people say; some that go a hunting in the woods, and some that live inside of trees, and some that have a comfortable home in fountains of water. We know nothing at all about them. We are three unfortunate old souls, that go wandering about in the dusk, and never had but one eye amongst us, and that one you have stolen away. Oh, give it back, good stranger! — whoever you are, give it back!"

All this while the Three Gray Women were groping with their outstretched hands, and trying their utmost to get hold of Perseus. But he took good care to keep out of their reach.

"My respectable dames," said he — for his mother had taught him always to use the greatest civility — "I hold your eye fast in my hand, and shall keep it safely for you, until you please to tell me where to find these Nymphs. The Nymphs, I mean, who keep the enchanted wallet, the flying slippers, and the what is it? — the helmet of invisibility."

"Mercy on us, sisters! what is the young man talking about?" exclaimed Scarecrow, Nightmare, and Shakejoint, one to another, with great appearance of astonishment. "A pair of flying slippers, quoth he! His heels would quickly fly higher than his head, if he were silly enough to put them on. And a helmet of invisibility! How could a helmet make him invisible, unless it were big enough for him to hide under it? And an enchanted wallet! What sort of a contrivance may that be, I wonder? No, no, good stranger! we can tell you nothing of these marvelous things. You have two eyes of your own, and we have but a single one amongst us three. You can find out such wonders better than three blind old creatures, like us."

Perseus, hearing them talk in this way, began really to think that the Gray Women knew nothing of the matter; and, as it grieved him to have put them to so much trouble, he was just on the point of restoring their eye and asking pardon for his rudeness in snatching it away. But Quicksilver caught his hand.

"Don't let them make a fool of you!" said he. "These Three Gray Women are the only persons in the world that can tell you where to find the Nymphs; and, unless you get that information, you will never succeed in cutting off the head of Medusa with the snaky locks. Keep fast hold of the eye, and all will go well."

As it turned out, Quicksilver was in the right. There are but few things that people prize so much as they do their eyesight; and the Gray Women valued their single eye as highly as if it had been half a dozen, which was the number they ought to have had. Finding that there was no other way of recovering it, they at last told Perseus what he wanted to know. No sooner had they done so, than he immediately, and with the utmost respect, clapped the eye into the vacant socket in one of their foreheads, thanked

them for their kindness, and bade them farewell. Before the young man was out of hearing, however, they had got into a new dispute, because he happened to have given the eye to Scarecrow, who had already taken her turn of it when their trouble with Perseus commenced.

It is greatly to be feared that the Three Gray Women were very much in the habit of disturbing their mutual harmony by bickerings of this sort; which was the more pity, as they could not conveniently do without one another, and were evidently intended to be inseparable companions. As a general rule, I would advise all people, whether sisters or brothers, old or young, who chance to have but one eye amongst them, to cultivate forbearance, and not all insist upon peeping through it at once.

Quicksilver and Perseus, in the meantime, were making the best of their way in quest of the Nymphs. The old dames had given them such particular directions, that they were not long in finding them out. They proved to be very different persons from Nightmare, Shakejoint, and Scarecrow; for, instead of being old, they were young and beautiful; and instead of one eye amongst the sisterhood, each Nymph had two exceedingly bright eyes of her own, with which she looked very kindly at Perseus. They seemed to be acquainted with Quicksilver; and, when he told them the adventure which Perseus had undertaken, they made no difficulty about giving him the valuable articles that were in their custody. In the first place, they brought out what appeared to be a small purse, made of deer skin, and curiously embroidered, and bade him be sure and keep it safe. This was the magic wallet. The Nymphs next produced a pair of shoes, or slippers, or sandals, with a nice little pair of wings at the heel of each.

"Put them on, Perseus," said Quicksilver. "You will find yourself as light-heeled as you can desire for the remainder of our journey."

So Perseus proceeded to put one of the slippers on, while he laid the other on the ground by his side. Unexpectedly, however, this other slipper spread its wings, fluttered up off the ground, and would probably have flown away, if Quicksilver had not made a leap, and luckily caught it in the air.

"Be more careful," said he, as he gave it back to Perseus. "It would frighten the birds, up aloft, if they should see a flying slipper amongst them."

When Perseus had got on both of these wonderful slippers, he was altogether too buoyant to tread on earth. Making a step or two, lo and behold! upward he popped into the air, high above the heads of Quicksilver and the Nymphs, and found it very difficult to clamber down again. Winged slippers, and all such high-flying contrivances, are seldom quite easy to manage until one grows a little accustomed to them. Quicksilver laughed at his companion's involuntary activity, and told him that he must not be in so desperate a hurry, but must wait for the invisible helmet.

The good-natured Nymphs had the helmet, with its dark tuft of waving plumes, all in readiness to put upon his head. And now there happened about as wonderful an incident as anything that I have yet told you. The instant before the helmet was put on, there stood Perseus, a beautiful young man, with golden ringlets and rosy cheeks, the crooked sword by his side, and the brightly polished shield upon his arm — a figure that seemed all made up of courage, sprightliness, and glorious light. But when the helmet had descended over his white brow, there was no longer any Perseus to be seen! Nothing but empty air! Even the helmet, that covered him with its invisibility, had vanished!

"Where are you, Perseus?" asked Quicksilver.

"Why, here, to be sure!" answered Perseus, very quietly, although his voice seemed to come out of the transparent atmosphere. "Just where I was a moment ago. Don't you see me?"

"No, indeed!" answered his friend. "You are hidden under the helmet. But, if I cannot see you, neither can the Gorgons. Follow me, therefore, and we will try your dexterity in using the winged slippers."

With these words, Quicksilver's cap spread its wings, as if his head were about to fly away from his shoulders; but his whole figure rose lightly into the air, and Perseus followed. By the time they had ascended a few hundred feet, the young man began to feel what a delightful thing it was to leave the dull earth so far beneath him, and to be able to flit about like a bird.

It was now deep night. Perseus looked upward, and saw the round, bright, silvery moon, and thought that he should desire nothing better than to soar up thither, and spend his life there. Then he looked downward again, and saw the earth, with its seas and lakes, and the silver courses of its rivers, and its snowy mountain peaks, and the breadth of its fields, and the dark cluster of its woods, and its cities of white marble; and, with the moonshine sleeping over the whole scene, it was as beautiful as the moon or any star could be. And, among other objects, he saw the island of Seriphus, where his dear mother was. Sometimes he and Quicksilver approached a cloud, that, at a distance, looked as if it were made of fleecy silver; although, when they plunged into it, they found themselves chilled and moistened with gray mist. So swift was their flight, however, that, in an instant, they emerged from the cloud into the moonlight again. Once, a high-soaring eagle flew right against the invisible Perseus. The bravest sights were the meteors, that gleamed suddenly out, as if a bonfire had been kindled in the sky, and made the moonshine pale for as much as a hundred miles around them.

As the two companions flew onward, Perseus fancied that he could hear the rustle of a garment close by his side; and it was on the side opposite to the one where he beheld Quicksilver, yet only Quicksilver was visible.

"Whose garment is this," inquired Perseus, "that keeps rustling close beside me in the breeze?"

"Oh, it is my sister's!" answered Quicksilver. "She is coming along with us, as I told you she would. We could do nothing without the help of my sister. You have no idea how wise she is. She has such eyes, too! Why, she can see you, at this moment, just as distinctly as if you were not invisible; and I'll venture to say, she will be the first to discover the Gorgons."

By this time, in their swift voyage through the air, they had come within sight of the great ocean, and were soon flying over it. Far beneath them, the waves tossed themselves tumultuously in mid-sea, or rolled a white surf-line upon the long beaches, or foamed against the rocky cliffs, with a roar that was thunderous, in the lower world; although it became a gentle murmur, like the voice of a baby half asleep, before it reached the ears of Perseus. Just then a voice spoke in the air close by him. It seemed to be a woman's voice, and was melodious, though not exactly what might be called sweet, but grave and mild.

"Perseus," said the voice, "there are the Gorgons."

"Where?" exclaimed Perseus. "I cannot see them."

"On the shore of that island beneath you," replied the voice. "A pebble, dropped from your hand, would strike in the midst of them."

"I told you she would be the first to discover them," said Quicksilver to Perseus. "And there they are!"

Straight downward, two or three thousand feet below him, Perseus perceived a small island, with the sea breaking into white foam all around its rocky shore, except on one side, where there was a beach of snowy sand. He descended towards it, and, looking earnestly at a cluster or heap of brightness, at the foot of a precipice of black rocks, behold, there were the terrible Gorgons! They lay fast asleep, soothed by the thunder of the sea; for it required a tumult that would have deafened everybody else to lull such fierce creatures into slumber. The moonlight glistened on their steely scales, and on their golden wings, which drooped idly over the sand. Their brazen claws, horrible to look at, were thrust out, and clutched the wave-beaten fragments of rock, while the sleeping Gorgons dreamed of tearing some poor mortal all to pieces. The snakes that served them instead of hair seemed likewise to be asleep; although, now and then, one would writhe, and lift its head, and thrust out its forked tongue, emitting a drowsy hiss, and then let itself subside among its sister snakes.

The Gorgons were more like an awful, gigantic kind of insect — immense, golden-winged beetles, or dragonflies, or things of that sort — at once ugly and beautiful — than like anything else; only that they were a thousand and a million times as big. And, with all this, there was something partly human about them, too. Luckily for Perseus, their faces were completely hidden from him by the posture in which they lay for, had he but looked one instant at them, he would have fallen heavily out of the air, an image of senseless stone.

"Now," whispered Quicksilver, as he hovered by the side of Perseus — "now is your time to do the deed! Be quick; for, if one of the Gorgons should awake, you are too late!"

"Which shall I strike at?" asked Perseus, drawing his sword and descending a little lower. "They all three look alike. All three have snaky locks. Which of the three is Medusa?"

It must be understood that Medusa was the only one of these dragon-monsters whose head Perseus could possibly cut off. As for the other two, let him have the sharpest sword that ever was forged, and he might have hacked away by the hour together, without doing them the least harm.

"Be cautious," said the calm voice which had before spoken to him. "One of the Gorgons is stirring in her sleep, and is just about to turn over. That is Medusa. Do not look at her! The sight would turn you to stone! Look at the reflection of her face and figure in the bright mirror of your shield."

Perseus now understood Quicksilver's motive for so earnestly exhorting him to polish his shield. In its surface he could safely look at the reflection of the Gorgon's face. And there it was — that

terrible countenance — mirrored in the brightness of the shield, with the moonlight falling over it, and displaying all its horror. The snakes, whose venomous natures could not altogether sleep, kept twisting themselves over the forehead. It was the fiercest and most horrible face that ever was seen or imagined, and yet with a strange, fearful, and savage kind of beauty in it. The eyes were closed, and the Gorgon was still in a deep slumber; but there was an unquiet expression disturbing her features, as if the monster was troubled with an ugly dream. She gnashed her white tusks, and dug into the sand with her brazen claws.

The snakes, too, seemed to feel Medusa's dream, and to be made more restless by it. They twined themselves into tumultuous knots, writhed fiercely, and uplifted a hundred hissing heads, without opening their eyes.

"Now, now!" whispered Quicksilver, who was growing impatient. "Make a dash at the monster!"

"But be calm," said the grave, melodious voice, at the young man's side. "Look in your shield, as you fly downward, and take care that you do not miss your first stroke."

Perseus flew cautiously downward, still keeping his eyes on Medusa's face, as reflected in his shield. The nearer he came, the more terrible did the snaky visage and metallic body of the monster grow. At last, when he found himself hovering over her within arm's length, Perseus uplifted his sword, while, at the same instant, each separate snake upon the Gorgon's head stretched threateningly upward, and Medusa unclosed her eyes. But she awoke too late. The sword was sharp; the stroke fell like a lightning-flash; and the head of the wicked Medusa tumbled from her body!

"Admirably done!" cried Quicksilver. "Make haste, and clap the head into your magic wallet."

To the astonishment of Perseus, the small, embroidered wallet, which he had hung about his neck, and which had hitherto been no bigger than a purse, grew all at once large enough to contain Medusa's head. As quick as thought, he snatched it up, with the snakes still writhing upon it, and thrust it in.

"Your task is done," said the calm voice. "Now fly; for the other Gorgons will do their utmost to take vengeance for Medusa's death."

It was, indeed, necessary to take flight; for Perseus had not done the deed so quietly but that the clash of his sword, and the hissing of the snakes, and the thump of Medusa's head as it tumbled upon the sea-beaten sand, awoke the other two monsters. There they sat, for an instant, sleepily rubbing their eyes with their brazen fingers, while all the snakes on their heads reared themselves on end with surprise, and with venomous malice against they knew not what. But when the Gorgons saw the scaly carcass of Medusa, headless, and her golden wings all ruffled, and half spread out on the sand, it was really awful to hear what yells and screeches they set up. And then the snakes! They sent forth a hundred-fold hiss, with one consent, and Medusa's snakes answered them out of the magic wallet.

No sooner were the Gorgons broad awake than they hurtled upward into the air, brandishing their brass talons, gnashing their horrible tusks, and flapping their huge wings so wildly, that some of the golden feathers were shaken out, and floated down upon the shore. And there, perhaps, those very feathers lie scattered, till this day. Up rose the Gorgons, as I tell you, staring horribly about, in hopes of turning somebody to stone. Had Perseus looked them in the face, or had he fallen into their clutches, his poor mother would never have kissed her boy again! But he took good care to turn his eyes another way; and, as he wore the helmet of invisibility, the Gorgons knew not in what direction to follow him; nor did he fail to make the best use of the winged slippers, by soaring upward a perpendicular mile or so. At that height, when the screams of those abominable creatures sounded faintly beneath him, he made a straight course for the island of Seriphus, in order to carry Medusa's head to King Polydectes.

I have no time to tell you of several marvellous things that befell Perseus, on his way homeward; such as his killing a hideous sea-monster, just as it was on the point of devouring a beautiful maiden; nor how he changed an enormous giant into a mountain of stone, merely by showing him the head of the Gorgon. If you doubt this latter story, you may make a voyage to Africa, some day or other, and see the very mountain, which is still known by the ancient giant's name.

Finally, our brave Perseus arrived at the island, where he expected to see his dear mother. But, during his absence, the wicked king had treated Danaë so very ill that she was compelled to make her escape, and had taken refuge in a temple, where some good old priests were extremely kind to her. These praiseworthy priests, and the kind-hearted fisherman, who had first shown hospitality to Danaë and little Perseus when he found them afloat in the chest, seem to have been the only persons on the island who cared about doing right. All the rest of the people, as well as King Polydectes himself, were remarkably ill-behaved, and deserved no better destiny than that which was now to happen.

Not finding his mother at home, Perseus went straight to the palace, and was immediately ushered into the presence of the king. Polydectes was by no means rejoiced to see him; for he had felt almost certain, in his own evil mind, that the Gorgons would have torn the poor young man to pieces, and have eaten him up, out of the way. However, seeing him safely returned, he put the best face he could upon the matter and asked Perseus how he had succeeded.

"Have you performed your promise?" inquired he. "Have you brought me the head of Medusa with the snaky locks? If not, young man, it will cost you dear; for I must have a bridal present for the beautiful Princess Hippodamia, and there is nothing else that she would admire so much."

"Yes, please your Majesty," answered Perseus, in a quiet way, as if it were no very wonderful deed for such a young man as he to perform. "I have brought you the Gorgon's head, snaky locks and all!"

"Indeed! Pray let me see it," quoth King Polydectes. "It must be a very curious spectacle, if all that travelers tell about it be true!"

"Your Majesty is in the right," replied Perseus. "It is really an object that will be pretty certain to fix the regards of all who look at it. And, if your Majesty think fit, I would suggest that a holiday be proclaimed, and that all your Majesty's subjects be summoned to behold this wonderful curiosity. Few of them, I imagine, have seen a Gorgon's head before, and perhaps never may again!"

The king well knew that his subjects were an idle set of reprobates, and very fond of sight-seeing, as idle persons usually are. So he took the young man's advice, and sent out heralds and messengers, in all directions, to blow the trumpet at the street-corners, and in the marketplaces, and wherever two roads met, and summon everybody to court. Thither, accordingly, came a great multitude of good-for-nothing vagabonds, all of whom, out of pure love of mischief, would have been glad if Perseus had met with some ill-hap in his encounter with the Gorgons. If there were any better people in the island (as I really hope there may have been, although the story tells nothing about any such), they stayed quietly at home, minding their business, and taking care of their little children. Most of the inhabitants, at all events, ran as fast as they could to the palace, and shoved, and pushed, and elbowed one another, in their eagerness to get near a balcony, on which Perseus showed himself, holding the embroidered wallet in his hand.

On a platform, within full view of the balcony, sat the mighty King Polydectes, amid his evil counselors, and with his flattering courtiers in a semicircle round about him. Monarch, counselors, courtiers, and subjects, all gazed eagerly towards Perseus.

"Show us the head! Show us the head!" shouted the people; and there was a fierceness in their cry as if they would tear Perseus to pieces, unless he should satisfy them with what he had to show. "Show us the head of Medusa with the snaky locks!"

A feeling of sorrow and pity came over the youthful Perseus.

"O King Polydectes," cried he, "and ye many people, I am very loath to show you the Gorgon's head!"

"Ah, the villain and coward!" yelled the people, more fiercely than before. "He is making game of us! He has no Gorgon's head! Show us the head, if you have it, or we will take your own head for a football!"

The evil counselors whispered bad advice in the king's ear; the courtiers murmured, with one consent, that Perseus had shown disrespect to their royal lord and master; and the great King Polydectes himself waved his hand, and ordered him, with the stern, deep voice of authority, on his peril, to produce the head.

"Show me the Gorgon's head, or I will cut off your own!"

And Perseus sighed.

"This instant," repeated Polydectes, "or you die!"

"Behold it, then!" cried Perseus, in a voice like the blast of a trumpet.

And, suddenly holding up the head, not an eyelid had time to wink before the wicked King Polydectes, his evil counselors, and all his fierce subjects were no longer anything but the mere images of a monarch and his people. They were all fixed, forever, in the look and attitude of that moment! At the first glimpse of the terrible head of Medusa, they whitened into marble! And Perseus thrust the head back into his wallet, and went to tell his dear mother that she need no longer be afraid of the wicked King Polydectes.

Tailypo

TRADITIONAL AMERICAN
FOLKTALE

An old man named Jeb used to live deep in the woods of West Virginia. His home was a dark, run-down log cabin. There was no running water or electricity. Old Man Jeb used to get his light and heat from a few lanterns and a big stone fireplace that was in the middle of the main room. He didn't like people; in fact, he preferred to live in the woods because there were no people around to bother him.

Old Man Jeb made his living as a hunter and trapper. He sold the furs of the animals he killed, and ate their meat. Occasionally, he would go into town in his ancient pickup truck to sell his furs and buy some basic supplies. But, for the most part, he kept pretty much to himself out in the woods.

The only company Old Man Jeb could stand was that of his three dogs: Shadrach, Meshach, and Abednigo. They slept under the front porch of his cabin. He would take them out hunting, shotgun in hand, and they would flush out and bring back game for him like deer and rabbits.

One winter was particularly hard for Old Man Jeb. Even

though he had stocked up on food and supplies, the season lasted unusually long, and he began to run low. Even worse, the animals that he normally hunted for fur to sell in town mysteriously began to disappear. With no furs to sell, no meat to eat, Old Man Jeb didn't even have money to buy store-bought food.

The first thing to run out was the meat. Old Man Jeb spent three long weeks eating turnip soup. He had nothing but rice to feed to his dogs. All three dogs began to get skinny and weak without any meat. But Old Man Jeb was too stubborn to ask any of the townsfolk for help.

One day, Old Man Jeb opened up the cupboard to get something to eat and realized there was nothing left at all. He absolutely had to find some meat. He picked up his shotgun, called his dogs Shadrach, Meshach, and Abednigo out from under the porch, and they all went out hunting in the snow. At first, things were depressingly the same as before; the dogs couldn't find the scent of so much as a thin old rabbit among the dead frosty underbrush. But then, just when Old Man Jeb decided to turn around and go back home to his dark log cabin, Meshach caught a scent on the breeze and barked loudly.

"Shadrach, Meshach, Abednigo! Go get 'im, boys!" Old Man Jeb shouted excitedly, raising his shotgun to his shoulder.

The dogs bounded away into a tangle of leafless bushes barking and snarling. Old Man Jeb steadied his gun, although the thought of meat for dinner already had his mouth watering and his hands were shaking in anticipation.

Suddenly, an animal sprang out of from the bushes and onto the path ahead of Old Man Jeb. He shot at it automatically. But even as he did so, his eyes told him that this thing wasn't like any animal he had ever seen before. It was the size of a cat, but had a long bushy tail, not like any cat Old Man Jeb had ever seen. It had rust-

colored fur, and when it paused just before Old Man Jeb shot at it, he caught sight of bright yellow eyes and sharp fangs. Something was telling him that he should be afraid of this creature, but he was so excited at the prospect of a good meal he hardly cared.

Old Man Jeb's heart fell when he saw the animal scamper away into the woods after his shot rang out in the forest. His dogs chased after it, still yelping. Old Man Jeb lowered his gun, thinking that he had missed the animal completely, but as he walked after the dogs he saw a big clump of fur lying on the path and he bent to pick it up. It was the creature's long, long tail.

"Shadrach, Meshach, Abednigo! Come back, boys!" Old Man Jeb called out, almost dancing for joy. The dogs came back whimpering at having to give up the chase. But when they saw the tail in Jeb's hand, they realized it meant food and they rolled on the ground, drooling and yipping happily.

As soon as he got back to the cabin, Old Man Jeb put a pot of water over the fire to boil. He skinned the tail and dropped it in the water, adding to it what few vegetables he had left in the cupboard to make a stew.

Soon the food was ready, and Old Man Jeb gobbled up almost the entire pot. When he was done, he threw the leftovers to the dogs under the porch, and they furiously fought over the bones.

Feeling full for the first time in weeks, Jeb went to bed content. But just as he was slipping into sleep he heard something outside, some distance from the cabin. It almost sounded like a voice, but it was unearthly. It was not a noise a human could utter. Old Man Jeb knew that no human would be foolish enough to wander in the woods at this late hour, anyway. The voice was soft. A chill ran down Old Man Jeb's spine as he heard:

Tailypo, tailypo. . .
All I want is my tailypo!

He jumped out of bed and ran out to the front porch in his pajamas. The dogs had heard the voice, too. They were scuffling and growling under the porch.

"Shadrach, Meshach, Abednigo! Go get 'im, boys!" Jeb ordered. The dogs leapt out from under the porch and ran off into the dark woods. Old Man Jeb listened for a while, but he didn't hear the voice again.

"Shadrach, Meshach, Abednigo! Come back, boys!" he called. He heard the snapping of twigs as the dogs returned. But only two dogs came out of the woods and ran under the porch. Shadrach did not return.

Now Old Man Jeb knew for sure that something wasn't right.

But there was no way he was going out into the woods in the middle of the night. He went back to bed and pulled the covers right up to his chin. He stared into the darkness.

It wasn't long before Old Man Jeb heard another noise. It was a scratching sound. Something was scratch, scratch, scratching on the outside walls of the log cabin. *Scraaaaaatch*, it went. Then he heard the voice again:

Tailypo, tailypo. . .
All I want is my tailypo!

Quaking, Old Man Jeb got out of his bed and rushed out to the porch.

"Meshach, Abednigo! Go get 'im, boys!" he yelled, his old voice cracking in fear.

The dogs bounded out from under the porch again and ran snarling around the side of the house. Old Man Jeb could hear barking and hissing as the dogs fought with the thing. Suddenly there was a yelp, and Abednigo came racing back around the shack and dove under the porch. Meshach was nowhere to be seen.

Terrified, Old Man Jeb ran back into the house and dove into his bed. This time he yanked the covers right up over his head.

It wasn't long before he heard the thing again. This time it sounded like it was right outside the door:

Tailypo, tailypo. . .
All I want is my tailypo!

From his bed, Old Man Jeb screamed, "Abednigo! Go get 'im, boy!" He heard a feral snarl, but he wasn't sure if it had come from the creature or from his dog.

The battle was fierce. There was the sound of ripping, snapping, and biting. Then there was silence.

Not for long, however. Old Man Jeb's heart hadn't even stopped racing when he heard:

Tailypo, tailypo. . .
Who has got my tailypo?

Now it sounded like the thing was right *inside* the cabin!

Old Man Jeb peeked out from under the covers. At the foot of his bed was the creature whose tail he had shot off. It was staring at him with its unnaturally bright yellow eyes. Its fangs dripped with blood.

Somehow, Old Man Jeb found his voice. He stammered, "I d-d-don't know w-w-who's got your t-t-tailyp-p-p-o."

"Yes, you do," the thing hissed. "YOU'VE GOT IT!"
And it leapt onto Old Man Jeb's chest and tore him to bits.

These days, if you ever dare to go out to the woods of West Virginia near sundown, some say you can still hear a voice on the wind softly chanting:

Tailypo, tailypo. . .
Now I've got my tailypo!

The Woodcutter's Wife

PRISCILLA GALLOWAY

The story that I intended to eat them is a fabrication. People will make up anything. I did intend to observe them closely under conditions of stress, and more blood would have been very useful to me.

In the end, I would probably have let them go back home. Their father, my husband, was making my life as wretched as his own. In the end, it would have been a choice between having the children back and pretending (for a while) to be a happy-ever-after fairy-tale family, or getting rid of all three of them and moving on.

Witchcraftly skill like mine has its drawbacks. When I take on human form, I age very little. In my true form, however, I am as old and hooknosed as they come, cheeks sunken, red eyes bleared, and rheumy. I'm tired, and getting more tired day by day. After the three hundredth birthday, there's not a lot one can do. All my power goes into keeping myself alive in my real form and maintaining my current transformation. Occasionally I find the energy to stir up a potion or weave a simple spell.

Does it seem strange that I have transformed to a poor woman, a woodcutter's wife? Wealth and power lose their charm when the novelty wears off. I've had my fill of both. In truth, a plain homespun dress and clogs take less energy than fancy silks covered with gold thread and pearls, and it's a smaller change from my real self to this middle-aged housewife than to a beautiful woman, be she old or young.

Besides, he was not poor when I married him: young, beautiful, and strong. Good too. They say opposites attract. His goodness appealed then, though that appeal quickly palled; the man has bored me to distraction these many years.

In an earlier transformation I went in for great beauty. I had a mirror to tell me so: a nice touch. Being beautiful is a full-time job, even with power such as mine was then. And do what one will, one gets older and loses it. My transformations must all age, however slowly. Eternal youth attracts much too much attention. I have nothing against age; experience accompanies it.

It was simpler being a woodcutter's wife than being a queen. My days were my own. When Karl went off to work in the forest with the children, I could adopt my real form and do some work of my own.

The most potent spells have always demanded human flesh or blood. Everyone knows about the Hand of Glory. It does indeed permit me to go at will into a house at night, certain that no sleeper shall awaken. But simply to cut off the hand of a hanged man is not enough. The hand is necessary, but not sufficient. It must be taken at a certain time and in a certain way and the spell cast truly. My Hand belonged to my husband the highwayman. We were together for ten happily eventful years a century ago. Then he cast his eyes toward a young gypsy woman. I did not wait for his unfaithfulness; next night the redcoats lay in wait for him. I have no energy to go far these years, but occasionally I would take his Hand from its hiding place and watch the slumber of Karl and the two children. Under its power they never stirred, but sometimes terror filled a face, or lips formed a soundless scream. When my need was great, I could draw off a cup of their blood, though not often. The children became pallid, and Karl could not work as vigorously as usual. No doubt this is partly why we became so desperately poor.

I watched our food dwindle almost to nothing, and did not act quickly enough. Without flesh to eat, I lacked the energy to transform. In my own shape, even though my eyes are dim, my nose is sharp. Odors float to me; then I can point at an animal and it comes to my oven. But at that time I was dependent on a loaf of bread and a jug of milk.

I remember snapping at the child, "Gretel, bring me that milk. Quickly, now!"

"Right away, Stepmother."

"Gretel, watch that broom!"

Too late. "Stupid child! Our last milk — and our last jug. A spoon, and here's a dish. Try and save some. Idiot child, I'll whip you till you bleed for this."

Hansel's voice behind me. "You're not our mother. You can't whip us. Only Dad."

I feel it all again. Rage flares in me, the power of anger. I must get away while this strength lasts. I must transform. They are not going to defy me and get away with it. Of course they don't follow me into the forest. Around the first bend in the path, I take my rightful form. Surely this rage will propel me safely to my little forest hut, where there is flesh to restore my strength. Come, my broom, it is not far to go.

Gretel did me a favor when she made me so angry. I must not forget again the power of rage. This stew has waited for me for six months. Under my spell it remained fresh and hot. How good it is.

I feel the blood in my veins. Energy! Power! I could have died in that stupid woman's body. I won't risk that again. But what to do?

Yes, the plan was forming. I could see it all. A few preparations and I'd be ready to go back.

"There's only bread for supper, Karl, and water to wash it down."

"I broke the jug, Daddy, and all the milk got spilled. I'm sorry, I'm sorry."

"Don't cry so hard, Gretel, love. I'll think of something. I love you. It was an accident, I know. Here, have some of my bread."

When I wasn't bored with Karl's goodness, I'd be furious. "She spilled the last drop of milk. We all have to go hungry. I said she couldn't have any bread."

"She's just a baby," Karl replied, holding out his whole piece. Gretel broke it carefully in half — she's a very precise child — and handed half back. They munched quite contentedly, as if we had a house full of food, and money to buy more.

I held back my rage and contemplated my plan. Admirable! After the children had gone to bed, Karl sat wearily staring into the fire. "I don't know what to do," he said. "Helga, what on earth are we going to do? I cut so little wood these days, and it's so far to town to sell it. If I had a horse to pull the cart, it would be easy — but if we had had a horse, we would have had to sell it or eat it long since. I don't know where to get food for the children."

That Karl! He didn't say anything about food for us! I made my face all soft and tender. "It's dreadful, Karl, dreadful. We can't sit by and see them starve to death. Us too, but we'll last longer than the children."

"I know. I can't bear it."

"I don't have any easy suggestion, Karl, and I can't solve it. We're all going to die. We have to accept that. The only thing I can think of is to make it quicker and easier for the little ones."

"Kill them?" His face was full of horror.

"No, no, of course not. We'll take them into the forest. We can build a big fire for them and leave them while we work, just like you always do. I'll go with you, Karl. If we take them far enough, they won't find their way back, and the end will be quick. I know it's horrible, dear husband, but I'm like you, I can't bear to watch them die."

I just looked at him, waiting for his will to crumble. I have eaten; he has not. My will is centuries strong.

"Tomorrow," he mumbled at last.

I slept well, but his side of the bed was tumbled and tossed; his face was gray as we got up and had our breakfast of water and a mouthful or two of bread.

"We're all going to the forest today," I said brightly. "Won't that be nice?"

Hansel looked at me. His eyes are very dark, almost black. Karl usually cuts his hair, but he has not done so lately, and dark curls frame Hansel's thin face. It was a considering look, almost judgmental it felt, but Hansel spoke evenly enough. "Yes, Stepmother," he said.

Karl and I led the party. Gretel was sobbing bitterly, almost as if she knew! But of course she couldn't know. "Come along, child," I said, in my best bracing-but-kind tone. "Hansel, why are you looking back?"

"I'm looking at a little bird sitting on the chimney," said Hansel. "It's almost as if it is trying to speak to me."

"Come along," I said, "move your legs." Karl said nothing. He has no talent for conversation.

The common story is right about what happened next. Hansel had indeed managed to overhear me talking to his father. While I slept, the brat had gone out and filled both pockets with white stones. We built the fire and left them, but they were back with the dawn the next day.

"Thank God," said Karl. "Thank God." He could say nothing else, but he hugged the thin bodies and his face shone through his tears.

"We'll come with you to town, Father," said Hansel. "I can help you pull the cart. Gretel can walk very well. She won't hold us up."

They came back in the evening laughing and crying by turns as they told me the story. In the market, a rich merchant had taken one look at Gretel and bought all the wood. He had his own servants pull the cart home while he took father and children to the tavern for a hot meal. Then he filled the cart with food: sacks of flour, meal, potatoes, a pail of honey, a box packed with meat, butter and eggs, jugs of milk and wine. Atop the load he set a crate

with six laying hens, who squawked and chattered when I set it down as if already they felt my eyes piercing their hearts.

"It's wonderful," I lied, cursing the man who had interfered with my plans, "but why on earth did a total stranger do all that?"

Karl's face grew solemn. "He told me his little daughter died not long ago. Gretel reminded him of her. He said she reminded him too much of how she looked before she died; he wanted Gretel to be healthy and well. 'Give her an egg every day,' he told us." Karl shook his head.

"It's a wonder he didn't want to keep her," I remarked.

"He did." Karl's voice was taut. "Yesterday I might have had a different answer. Food in your belly does make things look different, that's a fact. Today I told him nothing on earth would make me part with my darling. 'That's right,' said the merchant, 'that's just how I felt.' There were tears in his eyes. 'I would never come in the way of a father's love,' the man told me." Karl's arms tightened around Gretel; then he reached out to hug Hansel as well. "The merchant knew you needed food too," he said. "He thought you were a fine boy."

"So all's well that ends well," said I lightly, putting the big stewpot on the hob. "What a dinner we'll have!"

Next thing you know, they were dancing and singing in a circle, Karl bending to take the children's hands. Faster and faster they spun; I got tired and dizzy just looking. "Enough," I said, trying not to sound cross. "Gretel, you set the table. Hansel, bring more wood and then sweep the floor. Karl, you get Grandma's table cover out of the chest. Let's get ready for our feast."

The merchant's gift brought us luck. Nor did his kindness stop there. He sent a servant out to our hut the following day, leading a cow. "Milk for the little ones" was the message. The servant said his master did not want to see Gretel again, but he wanted all of us to be well and happy for her sake.

A witch learns patience in three hundred years. Hansel and Gretel fed the fowl and gathered the eggs. I milked the cow and churned the butter. Karl chopped wood and hauled it to town to sell. "I'll be able to get a horse and cart again, if this keeps up," he said, smiling. I kept up my energy and bided my time. When the children went with their father, it was easy to transform. I did not take any blood, except now and then a cup or so from the cow. Karl was cutting a lot more wood. "I've got my heart in it," said he, but I knew that good food and no blood loss were the reasons.

"A good heart," I told him, and so indeed he had. Bovine, banal, and good.

I bided my time.

First the cow dried up. "She needs freshening," said Karl. But we did not know anyone with a bull. So there was no more milk or butter. The hens gradually stopped laying. We had no rooster, so could never hatch any young. One by one the hens were stewed for dinner. The children wept. They had named the hens. The day we ate Patience, the last of them, I knew we were on the road to starvation again.

This time my plans were thorough. Food for me was hidden in the root cellar, under the sand. No chance this time that I would lack energy to transform. The stew was kept hot and fresh by one of my simpler spells, which also prevented any odor from leaking up to hungry noses.

Karl sold the cow. I told him he should go back to the merchant for more help, but he refused. "I'm no beggar, and you know it," he told me roughly. Yes, I knew, but I also knew he would have been thinking of it. After his words to me, he'd put it off awhile, even though Gretel was pale and thin. I needed time to go to town and arrange an accident. By the time Karl finally went to the merchant's house, the man had lain a month in his grave.

The price of the cow kept us through that winter, and Karl's woodcutting kept us through the following summer and fall. Then it was winter again, and again there came a day when we were down to our last jug of milk, our last loaf. Gretel did not drop the jug this time; with that one change, history repeated itself.

But this time I locked the door.

It was harder and at the same time easier to persuade Karl to abandon the children again in the forest. I wouldn't have thought any parent could become more besotted with a child than Karl had been already with Gretel, or prouder of a child than he had been of Hansel. He had taken to calling the day they returned the miracle day. "There were two miracles," he said. "The children found their way home. That's number one. And then all that wonderful food! Two miracles on the same day. Surely we are blessed, Helga," he would say. But not recently. He watched as the children again became pallid and gaunt, stared wordlessly as their laughter faded into silence.

"Yes," he said finally. "I cannot bear to see them suffer, Helga. It's worse than last time. I was so sure we were saved forever. This time it is harder. We will take them into the forest again. And this time we will take them deeper, as you say." He groaned. If I had been capable of pity, I might have pitied him then.

"Maybe there will be another miracle," I suggested.

Hope leapt in his eyes. "My very thought," he breathed. "Maybe a better miracle. Maybe."

As we set out the next morning, I paid more attention to Hansel than I had last time. Again he and Gretel lagged behind. Again Karl and I saw them turn to look back at the house. "What are you looking at now?" I asked at last. "It's getting late. It's hard enough to get a good load of wood without you holding us back."

"I'm just looking at the roof," Hansel replied. "Do you remember where my white cat used to sit, right beside the chimney? I'm thinking of her."

"Do you still miss her?" asked Karl. "Cats do just disappear sometimes, but it was very sad."

"Just as well," I said, remembering how that cat had fought as I twisted its neck, remembering the love potion I had made with its heart's blood. "Just as well, we couldn't have fed it anyway." We made our way onward in silence.

Again we lit a fire to keep the children warm. I set a little spell on a maple branch so that it would keep hitting an adjoining branch. To the children it would sound like an ax. They would be sure their father was not far away. Again we worked for part of the day, gradually making our way home.

Now that the children were gone, I could transform as soon as Karl had entered the forest. Every day I quickly flew the short distance by air to my hidden hut. I could see the children in the forest and could make an excellent guess as to when they would come across it as they wandered. They had never seen me in any form other than that of their stepmother. Even as a witch, I can put on a pleasant smile and warm manner when need arises.

The difficult part of my preparation was transforming the hut. None of the stories has ever done justice to my creativity. The windowpanes were of spun sugar, the story says. It does not add that they were a perfect one-way mirror. I could see out, but nobody could see in. The roof was gingerbread. It was a kind of gingerbread cake, with whipped cream on top. I didn't think the children would notice or care that there was no snow on the ground. The walls were sturdy gingerbread, with jujubes, jelly beans, and peppermint patties held on with icing. The doorsill and the door itself were blocks of chocolate. Inside, the cottage looked charming. It was charming — and charmed. I dreamed up the whole thing. Nobody ever built a gingerbread house before me.

It was a gigantic task, almost beyond my waning powers. All the spells I had stored over the years went to help build that sweet house. The result, no doubt of it at all, would be irresistible to a child.

I could hear them coming a long way off. I managed to waft the peppermint, chocolate, butterscotch, raspberry cheesecake smell of the place toward them. It worked! Minutes later, my little victims approached. Ha! I listened to them crunch and gnaw. At first they swallowed before they chewed. Later their manners became more civilized. When I thought they'd had enough to make them sick, I went out to give 'em hell for stealing my house.

"Sorry," said Gretel. Hansel remained silent. "We were starving," pleaded Gretel.

"That's no excuse," I began to say, and then realized I was saying exactly what their stepmother would say in such an event. I stopped in midbreath. My voice and form were so different that they'd never recognize me, but mannerisms, tone of voice might still betray.

"Come in," I invited. "I was just going to make tea."

"We can't stay, thank you," said Hansel politely. "We're not allowed."

"Thank you," said Gretel, with tears in her pretty blue eyes, "it's very kind of you." She followed me inside my chocolate door, and Hansel, scuffling his feet, followed unwillingly. "How beautiful," breathed Gretel, looking greedily around. Inside, the place was full of bright silks and brocades. I gave them delicate teas from cups of translucent china, along with food such as they had dreamed of but never eaten. Their eyes were closing as they ate, hunger and exhaustion warring in each scrawny body.

"This is better than the forest, isn't it?" I inquired as I led them to the bedroom. Four tired eyes rested longingly on two down-covered beds. Less than a minute later by the clock, both were

dead to the world. I wouldn't need my Hand of Glory if I wanted their blood. However, neither child had any blood to spare. I knew they would serve my purposes much better when they were rested and fed.

By morning my preparations for my young guests were complete. I asked Hansel to go into the stable to feed my horse. Then I clasped the padlock shut on the closed door. I did laugh when he tried to get out, though stories lie that say I cackled in glee. And certainly I did not bother to keep up the magic of the silk comforters. Let Gretel sleep with rags of blanket to keep her warm!

I really needed a servant to do all my work. My 313th birthday was coming up. I had every right to feel tired. Gretel was admirable. The smallest threat to Hansel sufficed. "That floor is still dirty. Scrub it again, or Hansel goes hungry tonight!" And the floor would be scrubbed until it sparkled. Actually I wanted to

fatten them both. I didn't want Hansel to miss any meals, but there was no real danger that I'd have to carry out my threats. Gretel was taking no chances at all.

The stories make me out an awful fool. "Hansel, stick your finger through the bars," they say I'd say, and Hansel would stick out a little bone. "Too thin to eat yet," they say I'd say, smiling a little with my withered mouth.

I don't like to look at my real face in the mirror. Most of my teeth are gone, and it takes energy to keep even a few false teeth in place with magic spells. That's why I eat stew these days: the meat is very soft. I have eaten human flesh, but not for more than a hundred years. Hansel was still young and tender, though not as tender as Gretel would be. But they could be killed and eaten only once. It would have been a very great waste. Alive and fat, they could supply blood for all the spells I would ever need.

Of course I knew Hansel was not sticking his finger out for me to feel. My eyesight is getting worse and worse, but my nose has not betrayed me, nor have my hands. My fingers know the difference between skin and bone.

All this time, I transformed at night and went home to be a loving wife to Karl. It added variety to my life to feed his guilt about the children, to put into his head subtle suggestions about animals, to nourish his nightmares. He stopped cutting wood and took to roaming the forest all day, looking and calling, returning exhausted at night, only to be exhausted even more by his horrid dreams. At what point would he be actually, irretrievably mad? I fed him twice a day, good meals, and he never even asked where the food was coming from, just ate weeping and slept with nightmares and went crying about the forest, never coming close to my little house; I made sure of that!

I had little philosophical conversations with Hansel. "What would happen if I ate you a little bit at a time? I could cut off one of your arms and begin on that. I am a witch, you know, Hansel, I could heal the stump and it wouldn't even bleed. Which arm would you like me to take first?"

Gretel only screamed and threw herself on the floor if I talked like that, and she was useless as a servant for several hours afterward, but Hansel would consider the topic gravely and reply evenly, as if it concerned him not at all, "I am sure I would not be good to eat. But you wouldn't need to take a whole arm to find that out. A piece of flesh would serve that purpose and leave me all my arms and legs. You might want me to do some heavy work for you sometime. I think you would want to make sure I am still able."

"We'll see," I'd say, and stomp off angrily. Of course I wanted him able to do the heavy work when needed. I wanted to enlarge my lab before winter, and it would be much easier on me for Hansel to construct it. My power continues, alas, to wane.

So that bit about the oven, and Gretel tricking me into it, that part is so much malarkey, as my Irish husband used to say. There was an oven, and I did have bread to bake, and I was teasing Gretel about baking Hansel in that oven, but I never told her to get into it to test it. That would be absurd. I had taken too much for granted, however. Gretel was not as submissive as she seemed. Wretched child!

How could she have managed to find the key to Hansel's padlock? The spell of invisibility ought to have lasted forever. Still, the day came when Hansel was not inside the stable but around the side of it, and the two of them did manage to push me inside and close the lock. Again a purple rage seized me. However, I was too well nourished to use its power well. I seized the bars. A

hundred years ago they would have given way like kindling. Now, however, they resisted me. I fell to the ground, overcome for the moment by my anger.

That must have been when the children pried open my jewel chest and filled their pockets. Likely they also took a satchel full of gems. My great topaz amulet was gone, along with the maharajah's emerald crown and the diamond of Zanzibar. I did not make a tally until much later, however. When I came to my senses, the children had fled and I was still imprisoned. If I transformed, I would lose my power. Should I change my transformation? A bird or insect or small animal could easily pass between the bars. However, I have energy to do this only once. Whatever transformation I take now, I'll have to keep for a long time, perhaps forever. What shall I do?

Could a skinny, scrawny child slip between these bars? How small would I have to be? Am I ready?

And if I do it, what then? Karl will have lost his wife. But the children will find him. They will have lots of food, and he roams the forest every day. They will find each other soon. If I become a small child, I won't be able to get very far. Luckily I do not want to go very far. My work is here, and I'm too old to start over. When I go to their door with big dark eyes and a hungry look, I know they will take me in.

The Ballad of Blasphemous Bill

ROBERT WILLIAM SERVICE

I took a contract to bury the body of blasphemous Bill MacKie,
Whenever, wherever or whatsoever
the manner of death he die —
Whether he die in the light o' day or
under the peak-faced moon;
In cabin or dance-hall, camp or dive,
mucklucks or patent shoon;
On velvet tundra or virgin peak, by glacier, drift, or draw;
In muskeg hollow or canyon gloom, by avalanche, fang, or claw;
By battle, murder, or sudden wealth,
by pestilence, hooch, or lead —
I swore on the Book I would follow and look
till I found my tombless dead.

For Bill was a dainty kind of cuss, and his mind was mighty sot
On a dinky patch with flowers and grass
in a civilized bone-yard lot.
And where he died or how he died, it didn't matter a damn
So long as he had a grave with frills and a tombstone "epigram."
So I promised him, and he paid the price in good cheechako coin
(Which the same I blowed in that very night
down in the Tenderloin).
Then I painted a three-foot slab of pine:
"Here lies poor Bill MacKie,"
And I hung it up on my cabin wall and I waited for Bill to die.

Years passed away, and at last one day
came a squaw with a story strange,
Of a long-deserted line of traps 'way back of the Bighorn range;
Of a little hut by the great divide, and a white man stiff and still,
Lying there by his lonesome self, and I figured it must be Bill.
So I thought of the contract I'd made with him,
and I took down from the shelf
The swell black box with the silver plate
he'd picked out for hisself;
And I packed it full of grub and "hooch,"
and I slung it on the sleigh;
Then I harnessed up my team of dogs and was off at dawn of day.

You know what it's like in the Yukon wild
when it's sixty-nine below;
When the ice-worms wriggle their purple heads
through the crust of the pale blue snow;

141

When the pine-trees crack like little guns
in the silence of the wood,
And the icicles hang down like tusks under the parka hood;
When the stove-pipe smoke breaks sudden off,
and the sky is weirdly lit,
And the careless feel of a bit of steel burns like a red-hot spit;
When the mercury is a frozen ball,
and the frost-fiend stalks to kill —
Well, it was just like that that day when I set out to look for Bill.

Oh, the awful hush that seemed to crush
me down on every hand,
As I blundered blind with a trail to find
through that blank and bitter land;
Half dazed, half crazed in the winter wild,
with its grim heart-breaking woes,
And the ruthless strife for a grip on life
that only the sourdough knows!
North by the compass, North I pressed;
river and peak and plain
Passed like a dream I slept to lose and I waked to dream again.

River and plain and mighty peak — and who could stand unawed?
As their summits blazed, he could stand undazed
at the foot of the throne of God.
North, aye, North, through a land accurst,
shunned by the scouring brutes,
And all I heard was my own harsh word
and the whine of the malamutes,

Till at last I came to a cabin squat, built in the side of a hill,
And I burst in the door, and there on the floor,
frozen to death, lay Bill.

Ice, white ice, like a winding-sheet,
　　sheathing each smoke-grimed wall;
Ice on the stove-pipe, ice on the bed, ice gleaming over all;
Sparkling ice on the dead man's chest, glittering ice in his hair,
Ice on his fingers, ice in his heart, ice in his glassy stare;
　　Hard as a log and trussed like a frog,
　　　　with his arms and legs outspread.
　　I gazed at the coffin I'd brought for him,
　　　　and I gazed at the gruesome dead,
And at last I spoke: "Bill liked his joke; but still, goldarn his eyes,
　　A man had ought to consider his mates
　　　　in the way he goes and dies."

Have you ever stood in an Arctic hut in the shadow of the Pole,
　With a little coffin six by three and a grief you can't control?
Have you ever sat by a frozen corpse that looks at you with a grin,
　　And that seems to say: "You may try all day,
　　　　but you'll never jam me in"?
　I'm not a man of the quitting kind, but I never felt so blue
　As I sat there gazing at that stiff and studying what I'd do.
　　Then I rose and I kicked off the husky dogs
　　　　that were nosing round about,
And I lit a roaring fire in the stove, and I started to thaw Bill out.

　　Well, I thawed and thawed for thirteen days,
　　　　but it didn't seem no good;
His arms and legs stuck out like pegs, as if they was made of wood.
Till at last I said: "It ain't no use — he's froze too hard to thaw;

He's obstinate, and he won't lie straight,
    so I guess I got to — *saw*."
So I sawed off poor Bill's arms and legs,
    and I laid him snug and straight
In the little coffin he picked hisself, with the dinky silver plate;
    And I came nigh near to shedding a tear
        as I nailed him safely down;
Then I stowed him away in my Yukon sleigh,
    and I started back to town.

So I buried him as the contract was in a narrow grave and deep,
    And there he's waiting the Great Clean-up,
        when the Judgment sluice-heads sweep;
    And I smoke my pipe and I meditate
        in the light of the Midnight Sun,
And sometimes I wonder if they *was*, the awful things I done.
    And as I sit and the parson talks, expounding of the Law,
I often think of poor old Bill — *and how hard he was to saw*.

The Haunted House

GEORGE MACDONALD

This must be the very night!
The moon knows it! — and the trees —
They stand straight upright,
Each a sentinel drawn up,
As if they dared not know
Which way the wind might blow!
The very pool, with dead gray eye,
Dully expectant, feels it nigh,
And begins to curdle and freeze!
And the dark night,
With its fringe of light,
Holds the secret in its cup!

II.
What can it be, to make
The poplars cease to shiver and shake,
And up in the dismal air
Stand straight and stiff as the human hair
When the human soul is dizzy with dread —
All but those two that strain

Aside in a frenzy of speechless pain,
Though never a wind sends out a breath
To tunnel the foggy rheum of death?
What can it be has power to scare
The full-grown moon to the idiot stare
Of a blasted eye in the midnight air?
Something has gone wrong;
A scream will come tearing out ere long!

III.
Still as death,
Although I listen with bated breath!
Yet something is coming, I know — is coming;
With an inward soundless humming,
Somewhere in me or in the air —
I cannot tell — but its foot is there!
Marching on to an unheard drumming,
Something is coming — coming —
Growing and coming;
And the moon is aware —
Aghast in the air
At the thing that is only coming
With an inward soundless humming,
And an unheard spectral drumming!

IV.
Nothing to see and nothing to hear!
Only across the inner sky
The wing of a shadowy thought flits by,
Vague and featureless, faceless, drear —
Only a thinness to catch the eye:

147

Is it a dim foreboding unborn,
Or a buried memory, wasted and worn
As the fading frost of a wintry sigh?
Anon I shall have it! — anon! — it draws nigh!
A night when—a something it was took place
That drove the blood from that scared moon-face!
Hark! was that the cry of a goat,
Or the gurgle of water in a throat?
Hush! there is nothing to see or hear,
Only a silent something is near;
No knock, no footsteps three or four,
Only a presence outside the door!
See! the moon is remembering — what?
The wail of a mother-left, lie-alone brat?
Or a raven sharpening its beak to peck?
Or a cold blue knife and a warm white neck?
Or only a heart that burst and ceased
For a man that went away released?
I know not — know not, but something is coming
Somehow back with an inward humming.

V.

Ha! Look there! Look at that house —
Forsaken of all things — beetle and mouse!
Mark how it looks! It must have a soul!
It looks, it looks, though it cannot stir;
See the ribs of it — how they stare!
Its blind eyes yet have a seeing air!
It *knows* it has a soul!
Haggard it hangs o'er the slimy pool,
And gapes wide open as corpses gape:

It is the very murderer!
The ghost has modelled himself to the shape
Of this drear house all sodden with woe,
Where the deed was done, long, long ago,
And filled with himself his new body full —
To haunt for ever his ghastly crime,
And see it come and go —
Brooding around it like motionless time,
With a mouth that gapes, and eyes that yawn
Blear and blintering and full of the moon,
Like one aghast at a hellish dawn.
— It is coming, coming soon!

VI.

For, ever and always, when round the tune
Grinds on the barrel of organ-time,
The deed is done; — and it comes anon —
True to the roll of the clock-faced moon,
True to the ring of the spheric chime,
True to the cosmic rhythm and rime;
Every point, as it first went on,
Will come and go till all is gone;
And palsied with horror from garret to core,
The house cannot shut its gaping door;
Its burst eye stares as if trying to see,
And it leans as if settling heavily,
Settling heavy with sickness dull:
It also is hearing the soundless humming
Of the wheel that is turning — the thing that is coming.
On the naked rafters of its brain,
Gaunt and wintred, see the train

Of gossiping, scandal-mongering crows,
That watch, all silent, with necks a-strain,
Wickedly knowing, with heads awry,
And the sharpened gleam of a cunning eye —
Watch, through the cracks of the ruined skull,
How the evil business goes!
— Beyond the eyes of the cherubim,
Beyond the ears of the seraphim,
Outside, forsaken, in the dim
Phantom-haunted chaos grim,
He stands with the deed going on in him!

VII.
O winds, winds! that lurk and peep
Under the edge of the moony fringe!
O winds, winds! up and sweep;
Up, and blow and billow the air,
Billow the air with blow and swinge;
Rend me this ghastly house of groans;
Rend and scatter the skeleton's bones
Over the deserts and mountains bare;
Blast and hurl and shiver aside
Nailed sticks and mortared stones;
Clear the phantom, with torrent and tide,
Out of the moon and out of my brain,
That the light may fall shadowless in again!

VIII.
But alas! then the ghost
O'er mountain and coast
Would go roaming, roaming; and never was swine,
That, grubbing and talking with snork and whine

On Gadarene mountains, had taken him in,
But would rush to the lake to unhouse the sin
For any charnel
This ghost is too carnal;
There is no volcano, burnt out and cold,
Whose very ashes are gray and old,
But would cast him forth in reviving flame,
To blister the sky with a smudge of shame.

IX.
Is there no help — none anywhere,
Under the earth, or above the air?
— Come, come, sad woman, whose tender throat
Has a red-lipped mouth that can sing no note!
Child, whose midwife, the third grim Fate,
Shears in hand, thy coming did wait!
Father, with blood-bedabbled hair!
Mother, all withered with love's despair!
Come, broken heart, whatever thou be,
Hasten to help this misery!
Thou wast only murdered, or left forlorn;
He is a horror, a hate, a scorn!
Come, if out of the holiest blue
That the sapphire throne shines through;
For pity come, though thy fair feet stand
Next to the elder-band;
Fling thy harp on the hyaline,
Hurry thee down the spheres divine;
Come, and drive those ravens away;
Cover his eyes from the pitiless moon;
Shadow his brain from her stinging spray;
Droop around him, a tent of love,

An odor of grace, a fanning dove;
Walk through the house with the healing tune
Of gentle footsteps; banish the shape
Remorse calls up, thyself to ape;
Comfort him, dear, with pardon sweet;
Cool his heart from its burning heat
With the water of life that lakes the feet
Of the throne of God, and the holy street.

X.

O God, he is but a living blot,
Yet he lives by thee — for if thou wast not,
They would vanish together, self-forgot,
He and his crime: — one breathing blown
From thy spirit on his would all atone,
Scatter the horror, and bring relief
In an amber dawn of holy grief:
God, give him sorrow; arise from within:
Art thou not in him, silence in din,
Stronger than anguish, deeper than sin?

XI.

Why do I tremble, a creature at bay!
'Tis but a dream — I drive it away.
Back comes my breath, and my heart again
Pumps the red blood to my fainting brain
Released from the nightmare's nine-fold train;
God is in heaven — yes, everywhere;
And Love, the all-shining, will kill Despair.
To the wall's blank eyeless space
I turn the picture's face.

XII.

But why is the moon so bare, up there?
And why is she so white?
And why does the moon so stare, up there —
Strangely stare, out of the night?
Why stand up the poplars
That still way?
And why do those two of them
Start astray?
And out of the black why hangs the gray?
Why does it hang down so, I say,
Over what house, like a fringed pall
Where the dead goes by in a funeral?
— Soul of mine,
Thou the reason canst divine: —
Into *thee* the moon doth stare
With pallid, terror-smitten air:
Thou, and the Horror lonely-stark,
Outcast of eternal dark,
Are in nature same and one,
And *thy* story is not done!
So let the picture face thee from the wall,
And let its white moon stare.

The Cedar Closet

LAFCADIO HEARN

I t happened ten years ago, and it stands out, and ever will stand out, in my memory like some dark, awful barrier dividing the happy, gleeful years of girlhood, with their foolish, petulant sorrows and eager, innocent joys, and the bright, lovely life which has been mine since. In looking back, that time seems to me shadowed by a dark and terrible brooding cloud, bearing in its lurid gloom what, but for love and patience the tenderest and most untiring, might have been the bolt of death, or, worse a thousand times, of madness. As it was, for months after "life crept on a broken wing," if not "through cells of madness," yet verily "through haunts of horror and fear." O, the weary, weary days and months when I longed piteously for rest! When sunshine was torture, and every shadow filled with horror unspeakable; when my soul's craving was for death; to be allowed to creep away from the terror which lurked in the softest murmur of the summer breeze, the flicker of the shadow of the tiniest leaf on the sunny grass, in every corner and curtain-fold in my dear old home. But love conquered all, and I can tell my story now, with awe and wonder, it is true, but quietly and calmly.

Ten years ago I was living with my only brother in one of the

155

quaint, ivy-grown, red-gabled rectories which are so picturesquely scattered over the fair breadth of England. We were orphans, Archibald and I; and I had been the busy, happy mistress of his pretty home for only one year after leaving school, when Robert Draye asked me to be his wife. Robert and Archie were old friends, and my new home, Draye's Court, was only separated from the parsonage by an old gray wall, a low iron-studded door in which admitted us from the sunny parsonage dawn to the old, old park which had belonged to the Drayes for centuries. Robert was lord of the manor; and it was he who had given Archie the living of Draye in the Wold.

It was the night before my wedding day, and our pretty home was crowded with the wedding guests. We were all gathered in the large old-fashioned drawing-room after dinner. When Robert left us late in the evening, I walked with him, as usual, to the little gate for what he called our last parting; we lingered awhile under the great walnut-tree, through the heavy, somber branches of which the September moon poured its soft pure light. With his last good-night kiss on my lips and my heart full of him and the love which warmed and glorified the whole world for me, I did not care to go back to share in the fun and frolic in the drawing-room, but went softly upstairs to my own room. I say "my own room," but I was to occupy it as a bedroom tonight for the first time. It was a pleasant south room, wainscoted in richly carved cedar, which gave the atmosphere a spicy fragrance. I had chosen it as my morning room on my arrival in our home; here I had read and sang and painted, and spent long, sunny hours while Archibald was busy in his study after breakfast. I had had a bed arranged there as I preferred being alone to sharing my own larger bedroom with two of my bridesmaids. It looked bright and cozy as I came in; my favorite low chair was drawn before the fire, whose rosy light

glanced and flickered on the glossy dark walls, which gave the room its name, "The Cedar Closet." My maid was busy preparing my toilet table, I sent her away, and sat down to wait for my brother, who I knew would come to bid me good-night. He came; we had our last fireside talk in my girlhood's home; and when he left me there was an incursion of all my bridesmaids for a "dressing-gown reception."

When at last I was alone I drew back the curtain and curled myself up on the low wide window-seat. The moon was at its brightest; the little church and quiet churchyard beyond the lawn looked fair and calm beneath its rays; the gleam of the white headstones here and there between the trees might have reminded me that life is not all peace and joy — that tears and pain, fear and parting, have their share in its story — but it did not. The tranquil happiness with which my heart was full overflowed in some soft tears which had no tinge of bitterness, and when at last I did lie down, peace, deep and perfect, still seemed to flow in on me with the moonbeams which filled the room, shimmering on the folds of my bridal dress, which was laid ready for the morning. I am thus minute in describing my last waking moments, that it may be understood that what followed was not creation of a morbid fancy.

I do not know how long I had been asleep, when I was suddenly, as it were, wrenched back to consciousness. The moon had set, the room was quite dark; I could just distinguish the glimmer of a clouded, starless sky through the open window. I could not see or hear anything unusual, but not the less was I conscious of an unwonted, a baleful presence near; an indescribable horror cramped the very beatings of my heart; with every instant the certainty grew that my room was shared by some evil being. I could not cry for help, though Archie's room was so close, and I knew that one call through the death-like stillness would bring him to me; all I could do was to gaze, gaze, gaze into the darkness. Suddenly — and a throb stung through every nerve — I heard distinctly from behind the wainscot against which the head of my bed was placed a low, hollow moan, followed on the instant by a cackling, malignant laugh from the other side of the room. If I had been one of the monumental figures in the little churchyard on which I had seen the quiet moonbeams shine a few hours before I could not have been more utterly unable to move or speak; every other faculty seemed to be lost in the one intent strain of eye and ear. There came at last the sound of a halting step, the tapping of a crutch upon the floor, then stillness, and slowly, gradually the room filled with light — a pale, cold, steady light. Everything around was exactly as I had last seen it in the mingled shine of the moon and fire, and though I heard at intervals the harsh laugh, the curtain at the foot of the bed hid from me whatever uttered it.

Again, low but distinct, the piteous moan broke forth, followed by some words in a foreign tongue, and with the sound a figure started from behind the curtain — a dwarfed, deformed woman, dressed in a loose robe of black, sprinkled with golden stars, which gave forth a dull, fiery gleam, in the mysterious light; one lean, yellow hand clutched the curtain of my bed; it glittered with jeweled rings; — long black hair fell in heavy masses from a golden circlet over the stunted form. I saw it all clearly as I now see the pen which writes these words and the hand which guides it. The face was turned from me, bent aside, as if greedily drinking in those astonished moans; I noted even the streaks of gray in the long tresses, as I lay helpless in dumb, bewildered horror.

"Again!" she said hoarsely, as the sounds died away into indistinct murmurs, and advancing a step she tapped sharply with a crutch on the cedar wainscot; then again louder and more purposeful rose the wild beseeching voice; this time the words were English.

"Mercy, have mercy! not on me, but on my child, my little one; she never harmed you. She is dying — she is dying here in darkness; let me but see her face once more. Death is very near, nothing can save her now; but grant one ray of light, and I will pray that you may be forgiven, if forgiveness there be for such as you."

"What, you kneel at last! Kneel to Gerda, and kneel in vain. A ray of light; Not if you could pay for it in diamonds. You are mine! Shriek and call as you will, no other ears can hear. Die together. You are mine to torture as I will; mine, mine, mine!" and again an awful laugh rang through the room. At the instant she turned. O the face of malign horror that met my gaze! The green eyes flamed, and with something like the snarl of a savage beast she sprang toward me; that hideous face almost touched mine; the grasp of the skinny jeweled hand was all but on me; then — I suppose I fainted.

For weeks I lay in brain fever, in mental horror and weariness so intent, that even now I do not like to let my mind dwell on it. Even when the crisis was safely past I was slow to rally; my mind was utterly unstrung. I lived in a world of shadows. And so winter wore by, and brought us to the fair spring morning when at last I stood by Robert's side in the old church, a cold, passive, almost unwilling bride. I cared neither to refuse nor consent to anything that was suggested; so Robert and Archie decided for me, and I allowed them to do with me as they would, while I brooded silently and ceaselessly on the memory of that terrible night. To my husband I told all one morning in a sunny Bavarian valley, and my weak, frightened mind drew strength and peace from his; by degrees the haunting horror wore away, and when we came home for a happy reason nearly two years afterward, I was as strong and blithe as in my girlhood. I had learned to believe that it had all been, not the cause, but the commencement of my fever. I was to be undeceived.

Our little daughter had come to us in the time of roses; and now Christmas was with us, our first Christmas at home, and the house was full of guests. It was a delicious old-fashioned Yule; plenty of skating and outdoor fun, and no lack of brightness indoors. Toward New Year a heavy fall of snow set in which kept us all prisoners; but even then the days flew merrily, and somebody suggested tableaux for the evenings. Robert was elected manager; there was a debate and selection of subjects, and then came the puzzle of where, at such short notice, we could procure the dresses required. My husband advised a raid on some mysterious oaken chests which he knew had been for years stowed away in a turret-room. He remembered having, when a boy, seen the housekeeper inspecting them, and their contents

had left a hazy impression of old stand-alone brocades, gold tissues, sacques, hoops, and hoods, the very mention of which put us in a state of wild excitement. Mrs. Moultrie was summoned, looked duly horrified at the desecration of what to her were relics most sacred; but seeing it was inevitable, she marshaled the way, a protest in every rustle and fold of her stiff silk dress.

"What a charming old place," was the exclamation with variations as we entered the long oak-joisted room, at the further end of which stood in goodly array the chests whose contents we coveted. Bristling with unspoken disapproval, poor Mrs. Moultrie unlocked one after another, and then asked permission to retire, leaving us unchecked to "cry havoc." In a moment the floor was covered with piles of silks and velvets.

"Meg," cried little Janet Crawford, dancing up to me, "isn't it a good thing to live in the age of tulle and summer silks? Fancy being imprisoned for life in a fortress like this!" holding up a thick crimson and gold brocade, whale-boned and buckramed at all points. It was thrown aside, and she half lost herself in another chest and was silent. Then — "Look, Major Fraudel. This is the very thing for you — a true astrologer's robe, all black velvet and golden stars. If it were but long enough; it just fits me."

I turned and saw — the pretty slight figure, the innocent girlish face dressed in the robe of black and gold, identical in shape, pattern and material with what I too well remembered. With a wild cry I hid my face and cowered away.

"Take it off! O, Janet — Robert — take it from her!"

Every one turned wondering. In an instant my husband saw, and catching up the cause of my terror, flung it hastily into the chest again, and lowered the lid. Janet looked half offended, but the cloud passed in an instant when I kissed her, apologizing as well as I could. Rob laughed at us both, and voted an adjournment to a warmer room, where we could have the chests brought to us to ransack at leisure. Before going down, Janet and I went into a small anteroom to examine some old pictures which leaned against the wall.

"This is just the thing, Jennie, to frame the tableaux," I said, pointing to an immense frame, at least twelve feet square. "There is a picture in it," I added, pulling back the dusty folds of a heavy curtain which fell before it.

"That can be easily removed," said my husband, who had followed us.

With his assistance we drew the curtain quite away, and in the now fast waning light could just discern the figure of a girl in white against a dark background. Robert rang for a lamp, and when it came we turned with much curiosity to examine the painting, as to the subject of which we had been making odd merry guesses while we waited. The girl was young, almost childish — very lovely, but, oh, how sad! Great tears stood in the innocent eyes and on the round young cheeks, and her hands were clasped tenderly around the arms of a man who was bending toward her, and, did I dream? — no, there in hateful distinctness was the hideous woman of the Cedar Closet — the same in every distorted line, even to the starred dress and golden circlet. The swarthy hues of the dress and face had at first caused us to overlook her. The same wicked eyes seemed to glare into mine. After one wild bound my heart seemed to stop its beating, and I knew no more. When I recovered from a long, deep swoon, great lassitude and intense nervous excitement followed; my illness broke up the party, and for months I was an invalid. When again Robert's love and patience had won me back to my old health and happiness, he told me all the truth, so far as it had been preserved in old records of the family.

It was in the sixteenth century that the reigning lady of Draye Court was a weird, deformed woman, whose stunted body, hideous face, and a temper which taught her to hate and vilify everything good and beautiful for the contrast offered to herself, made her universally feared and disliked. One talent only she possessed; it was for music; but so wild and strange were the strains she drew from the many instruments of which she was mistress, that the gift only intensified the dread with which she was regarded. Her father had died before her birth; her mother did not survive it; near relatives she had none; she had lived her lonely, loveless life from youth to middle age. When a young girl came to the Court, no one knew more than that she was a poor relation. The dark woman seemed to look more kindly on this young cousin than on any one that had hitherto crossed her somber path, and indeed so great was the charm which Marian's goodness, beauty and innocent gayety exercised on every one that the servants ceased to marvel at her having gained the favor of their gloomy mistress. The girl seemed to feel a kind of wondering, pitying affection for the unhappy woman; she looked on her through an atmosphere created by her own sunny nature, and for a time all went well. When Marian had been at the Court for a year, a foreign musician appeared on the scene. He was a Spaniard, and had been engaged by Lady Draye to build for her an organ said to be of fabulous power and sweetness. Through long bright summer days he and his employer were shut up together in the music room — he busy in the construction of the wonderful instrument, she aiding and watching his work. These days were spent by Marian in various ways — pleasant idleness and pleasant work, long canters on her chestnut pony, dreamy mornings by the brook with rod and line, or in the village near, where she found a welcome everywhere. She played with the children, nursed the

babies, helped the mothers in a thousand pretty ways, gossiped with old people, brightening the day for everybody with whom she came in contact. Then in the evening she sat with Lady Draye and the Spaniard in the saloon talking in that soft foreign tongue which they generally used. But this was but the music between the acts; the terrible drama was coming. The motive was of course the same as that of every life drama which has been played out from the old, old days when the curtain rose upon the garden scene of Paradise. Philip and Marian loved each other, and having told their happy secret to each other, they, as in duty bound, took it to their patroness. They found her in the music room. Whether the glimpses she caught of a beautiful world from which she was shut out maddened her, or whether she, too, loved the foreigner, was never certainly known; but through the closed door passionate words were heard, and very soon Philip came out alone, and left the house without a farewell to any in it. When the servants did at last venture to enter, they found Marian lifeless on the floor, Lady Draye standing over her with crutch uplifted, and blood flowing from a wound in the girl's forehead. They carried her away and nursed her tenderly; their mistress locked the door as they left, and all night long remained alone in darkness. The music which came out without pause on the still night air was weird and wicked beyond any strains which had ever before flowed even from beneath her fingers; it ceased with morning light; and as the day wore on it was found that Marian had fled during the night, and that Philip's organ had sounded its last strain — Lady Draye had shattered and silenced it forever. She never seemed to notice Marian's absence and no one dared to mention her name. Nothing was ever known certainly of her fate; it was supposed that she had joined her lover.

Years passed, and with each Lady Draye's temper grew fiercer

and more malevolent. She never quitted her room unless on the anniversary of that day and night, when the tapping of her crutch and high-heeled shoes was heard for hours as she walked up and down the music room, which was never entered save for this yearly vigil. The tenth anniversary came round, and this time the vigil was not unshared. The servants distinctly heard the sound of a man's voice mingling in earnest conversation with her shrill tones; they listened long, and at last one of the boldest ventured to look in, himself unseen. He saw a worn, traveled-stained man; dusty, foot-sore, poorly dressed, he still at once recognized the handsome, gay Philip of ten years ago. He held in his arms a little sleeping girl; her long curls, so like poor Marian's, strayed over his shoulder. He seemed to be pleading in that strange musical tongue for the little one; for as he spoke he lifted, O, so tenderly, the cloak which partly concealed her, and showed the little face, which he doubtless thought might plead for itself. The woman, with a furious gesture, raised her crutch to strike the child; he stepped quickly backward, stooped to kiss the little girl, then, without a word, turned to go. Lady Draye called on him to return with an imperious gesture, spoke a few words, to which he seemed to listen gratefully, and together they left the house by the window which opened on the terrace. The servants followed them, and found she led the way to the parsonage, which was at the time unoccupied. It was said that he was in some political danger as well as in deep poverty, and that she had hidden him here until she could help him to a better asylum. It was certain that for many nights she went to the parsonage and returned before dawn, thinking herself unseen. But one morning she did not come home; her people consulted together; her relenting toward Philip had made them feel more kindly toward her than ever before; they sought her at the parsonage and found her lying across its threshold dead, a vial clasped in her rigid fingers. There was no sign of the late presence of Philip and his child; it was believed she had sped them on their way before she killed herself. They laid her in a suicide's grave. For more than fifty years after the parsonage was shut up. Though it had been again inhabited no one had ever been terrified by the specter I had seen; probably the Cedar Closet had never before been used as a bedroom.

Robert decided on having the wing containing the haunted room pulled down and rebuilt, and in doing so the truth of my story gained a horrible confirmation. When the wainscot of the Cedar Closet was removed a recess was discovered in the massive old wall, and in this lay moldering fragments of the skeletons of a man and child!

There could be but one conclusion drawn, the wicked woman had imprisoned them there under pretense of hiding and helping

them; and once they were completely at her mercy, had come night after night with unimaginable cruelty to gloat over their agony, and, when that long anguish was ended, ended her odious life by a suicide's death. We could learn nothing of the mysterious painting. Philip was an artist, and it may have been his work. We had it destroyed, so that no record of the terrible story might remain. I have no more to add, save that but for those dark days left by Lady Draye as a legacy of fear and horror, I should never have known so well the treasure I hold in the tender, unwearying, faithful love of my husband — known the blessing that every sorrow carries in its heart, that

> "Every cloud that spreads above
> And veileth love, itself is love."

The Miser in the Bush

THE BROTHERS GRIMM

A farmer had a faithful and diligent servant, who had worked hard for him three years, without having been paid any wages. At last it came into the man's head that he would not go on thus without pay any longer; so he went to his master, and said, "I have worked hard for you a long time, I will trust to you to give me what I deserve to have for my trouble." The farmer was a sad miser, and knew that his man was very simple-hearted; so he took out threepence, and gave him for every year's service a penny. The poor fellow thought it was a great deal of money to have, and said to himself, "Why should I work hard, and live here on bad fare any longer? I can now travel into the wide world, and make myself merry." With that he put his money into his purse, and set out, roaming over hill and valley.

As he jogged along over the fields, singing and dancing, a little dwarf met him, and asked him what made him so merry. "Why, what should make me down-hearted?" said he; "I am sound in health and rich in purse, what should I care for? I have saved up my three years' earnings and have it all safe in my pocket." "How much may it come to?" said the little man. "Full threepence," replied the countryman. "I wish you would give them to me," said the other; "I am very poor." Then the man pitied him, and gave him all he had; and the little dwarf said in return, "As you have such a kind honest heart, I will grant you three wishes — one for every penny; so choose whatever you like." Then the countryman rejoiced at his good luck, and said, "I like many things better than money: first, I will have a bow that will bring down everything I shoot at; secondly, a fiddle that will set everyone dancing that hears me play upon it; and thirdly, I should like that everyone should grant what I ask." The dwarf said he should have his three wishes; so he gave him the bow and fiddle, and went his way.

Our honest friend journeyed on his way too; and if he was merry before, he was now ten times more so. He had not gone far before he met an old miser: close by them stood a tree, and on the topmost twig sat a thrush singing away most joyfully. "Oh, what a pretty bird!" said the miser; "I would give a great deal of money to have such a one." "If that's all," said the countryman, "I will soon bring it down." Then he took up his bow, and down fell the thrush into the bushes at the foot of the tree. The miser crept into the bush to find it; but directly he had got into the middle, his companion took up his fiddle and played away, and the miser began to dance and spring about, capering higher and higher in the air. The thorns soon began to tear his clothes till they all hung in rags about him, and he himself was all scratched and wounded, so that the blood ran down. "Oh, for heaven's sake!" cried the miser, "Master! master! pray let the fiddle alone. What have I done to deserve this?" "Thou hast shaved many a poor soul close enough," said the other; "thou art only meeting thy reward": so he played up another tune. Then the miser began to beg and promise, and offered money for his

liberty; but he did not come up to the musician's price for some time, and he danced him along brisker and brisker, and the miser bid higher and higher, till at last he offered a round hundred of florins that he had in his purse, and had just gained by cheating some poor fellow. When the countryman saw so much money, he said, "I will agree to your proposal." So he took the purse, put up his fiddle, and traveled on very pleased with his bargain.

Meanwhile the miser crept out of the bush half-naked and in a piteous plight, and began to ponder how he should take his revenge, and serve his late companion some trick. At last he went to the judge, and complained that a rascal had robbed him of his money, and beaten him into the bargain; and that the fellow who did it carried a bow at his back and a fiddle hung round his neck. Then the judge sent out his officers to bring up the accused wherever they should find him; and he was soon caught and brought up to be tried.

The miser began to tell his tale, and said he had been robbed of his money. "No, you gave it me for playing a tune to you." said the countryman; but the judge told him that was not likely, and cut the matter short by ordering him off to the gallows.

So away he was taken; but as he stood on the steps he said, "My Lord Judge, grant me one last request." "Anything but thy life," replied the other. "No," said he, "I do not ask my life; only to let me play upon my fiddle for the last time." The miser cried out, "Oh, no! no! for heaven's sake don't listen to him! don't listen to him!" But the judge said, "It is only this once, he will soon have done." The fact was, he could not refuse the request, on account of the dwarf's third gift.

Then the miser said, "Bind me fast, bind me fast, for pity's sake." But the countryman seized his fiddle, and struck up a tune, and at the first note judge, clerks, and jailer were in motion; all began capering, and no one could hold the miser. At the second note the hangman let his prisoner go, and danced also, and by the time he had played the first bar of the tune, all were dancing together — judge, court, and miser, and all the people who had followed to look on. At first the thing was merry and pleasant enough; but when it had gone on a while, and there seemed to be no end of playing or dancing, they began to cry out, and beg him to leave off; but he stopped not a whit the more for their entreaties, till the judge not only gave him his life, but promised to return him the hundred florins.

Then he called to the miser, and said, "Tell us now, you vagabond, where you got that gold, or I shall play on for your amusement only," "I stole it," said the miser in the presence of all the people; "I acknowledge that I stole it, and that you earned it fairly." Then the countryman stopped his fiddle, and left the miser to take his place at the gallows.

"Q." a psychic pstory of the psupernatural

STEPHEN LEACOCK

I cannot expect that any of my readers will believe the story which I am about to narrate. Looking back upon it, I scarcely believe it myself. Yet my narrative is so extraordinary and throws such light upon the nature of our communications with beings of another world, that I feel I am not entitled to withhold it from the public.

I had gone over to visit Annerly at his rooms. It was Saturday, October 31. I remember the date so precisely because it was my pay day, and I had received six sovereigns and ten shillings. I remembered the sum so exactly because I had put the money into my pocket, and I remember into which pocket I had put it because I had no money in any other pocket. My mind is perfectly clear on all these points.

Annerly and I sat smoking for some time.

Then quite suddenly —

"Do you believe in the supernatural?" he asked.

I started as if I had been struck.

At the moment when Annerly spoke of the supernatural I had been thinking of something entirely different. The fact that he should speak of it at the very instant when I was thinking of something else, struck me as at least a very singular coincidence.

For a moment I could only stare.

"What I mean is," said Annerly, "do you believe in phantasms of the dead?"

"Phantasms?" I repeated.

"Yes, phantasms, or if you prefer the word, phanograms, or say if you will phanogrammatical manifestations, or more simply psychophantasmal phenomena?"

I looked at Annerly with a keener sense of interest than I had ever felt in him before. I felt that he was about to deal with events and experiences of which in the two or three months that I had known him he had never seen fit to speak.

I wondered now that it had never occurred to me that a man whose hair at fifty-five was already streaked with gray, must have passed through some terrible ordeal.

Presently, Annerly spoke again.

"Last night I saw Q," he said.

"Good heavens!" I ejaculated. I did not in the least know who Q was, but it struck me with a thrill of indescribable terror that Annerly had seen Q. In my own quiet and measured existence such a thing had never happened.

"Yes," said Annerly, "I saw Q as plainly as if he were standing here. But perhaps I had better tell you something of my past relationship with Q, and you will understand exactly what the present situation is."

Annerly seated himself in a chair on the other side of the fire from me, lighted a pipe and continued.

"When first I knew Q he lived not very far from a small town in the south of England, which I will call X, and was betrothed to a beautiful and accomplished girl whom I will name M."

Annerly had hardly begun to speak before I found myself listening with riveted attention. I realized that it was no ordinary experience that he was about to narrate. I more than suspected that Q and M were not the real names of his unfortunate acquaintances, but were in reality two letters of the alphabet selected almost at random to disguise the names of his friends. I was still pondering over the ingenuity of the thing when Annerly went on:

"When Q and I first became friends, he had a favorite dog which, if necessary, I might name Z, and which followed him in and out of X on his daily walk."

"In and out of X," I repeated in astonishment.

"Yes," said Annerly, "in and out."

My senses were now fully alert. That Z should have followed Q out of X, I could readily understand, but that he should first have followed him in seemed to pass the bounds of comprehension.

"Well," said Annerly, "Q and Miss M were to be married. Everything was arranged. The wedding was to take place on the last day of the year. Exactly six months and four days before the appointed day (I remember the date because the coincidence struck me as peculiar at the time), Q came to me late in the evening in great distress. He had just had, he said, a premonition of his own death. That evening, while sitting with Miss M on the verandah of her house, he had distinctly seen a projection of the dog R pass along the road."

"Stop a moment," I said. "Did you not say that the dog's name was Z?"

Annerly frowned slightly.

"Quite so," he replied. "Z, or more correctly Z R, since Q was in the habit, perhaps from motives of affection, of calling him R as well as Z. Well, then, the projection, or phanogram, of the dog passed in front of them so plainly that Miss M swore that she could have believed that it was the dog himself. Opposite the house the phantasm stopped for a moment and wagged its tail. Then it passed on, and quite suddenly disappeared around the corner of a stone wall, as if hidden by the bricks. What made the thing still more mysterious was that Miss M's mother, who is partially blind, had only partially seen the dog."

Annerly paused a moment. Then he went on:

"This singular occurrence was interpreted by Q, no doubt correctly, to indicate his own approaching death. I did what I could to remove this feeling, but it was impossible to do so, and he presently wrung my hand and left me, firmly convinced that he would not live till morning."

"Good heavens!" I exclaimed, "and he died that night?"

"No, he did not," said Annerly quietly, "that is the inexplicable part of it."

"Tell me about it," I said.

"He rose that morning as usual, dressed himself with his customary care, omitting none of his clothes, and walked down to his office at the usual hour. He told me afterwards that he remembered the circumstances so clearly from the fact that he had gone to the office by the usual route instead of taking any other direction."

"Stop a moment," I said. "Did anything unusual happen to mark that particular day?"

"I anticipated that you would ask that question," said Annerly, "but as far as I can gather, absolutely nothing happened. Q returned from his work, and ate his dinner apparently much as usual, and presently went to bed complaining of a slight feeling of drowsiness, but nothing more. His stepmother, with whom he lived, said afterwards that she could hear the sound of his breathing quite distinctly during the night."

"And did he die that night?" I asked, breathless with excitement.

"No," said Annerly, "he did not. He rose the next morning feeling about as before except that the sense of drowsiness had apparently passed, and that the sound of his breathing was no longer audible."

Annerly again fell into silence. Anxious as I was to hear the rest of his astounding narrative, I did not like to press him with questions. The fact that our relations had hitherto been only of a formal character, and that this was the first occasion on which he had invited me to visit him at his rooms, prevented me from assuming too great an intimacy.

"Well," he continued, "Q went to his office each day after that with absolute regularity. As far as I can gather there was nothing either in his surroundings or his conduct to indicate that any peculiar fate was impending over him. He saw Miss M regularly, and the time fixed for their marriage drew nearer each day."

"Each day?" I repeated in astonishment.

"Yes," said Annerly, "every day. For some time before his marriage I saw but little of him. But two weeks before that event was due to happen, I passed Q one day in the street. He seemed for a moment about to stop, then he raised his hat, smiled and passed on."

"One moment," I said, "if you will allow me a question that seems of importance — did he pass on and then smile and raise his hat, or did he smile into his hat, raise it, and then pass on afterwards?"

"Your question is quite justified," said Annerly, "though I think I can answer with perfect accuracy that he first smiled, then stopped smiling and raised his hat, and then stopped raising his hat and passed on."

"However," he continued, "the essential fact is this: on the day appointed for the wedding, Q and Miss M were duly married."

"Impossible!" I gasped; "duly married, both of them?"

"Yes," said Annerly, "both at the same time. After the wedding Mr. and Mrs. Q —"

"Mr. and Mrs. Q," I repeated in perplexity.

"Yes," he answered, "Mr. and Mrs. Q — for after the wedding Miss M took the name of Q — left England and went out to Australia, where they were to reside."

"Stop one moment," I said, "and let me be quite clear — in going out to settle in Australia it was their intention to reside there?"

"Yes," said Annerly, "that at any rate was generally understood. I myself saw them off on the steamer, and shook hands with Q, standing at the same time quite close to him."

"Well," I said, "and since the two Q's, as I suppose one might almost call them, went to Australia, have you heard anything from them?"

"That," replied Annerly, "is a matter that has shown the same singularity as the rest of my experience. It is now four years since Q and his wife went to Australia. At first I heard from him quite regularly, and received two letters each month. Presently I only received one letter every two months, and later two letters every six months, and then only one letter every twelve months. Then until last night I heard nothing whatever of Q for a year and a half."

I was now on the tiptoe of expectancy.

"Last night," said Annerly very quietly, "Q appeared in this room, or rather, a phantasm or psychic manifestation of him. He seemed in great distress, made gestures which I could not understand, and kept turning his trouser pockets inside out. I was too spellbound to question him, and tried in vain to divine his meaning. Presently the phantasm seized a pencil from the table, and wrote the words, 'Two sovereigns, tomorrow night, urgent.'"

Annerly was again silent. I sat in deep thought. "How do you interpret the meaning which Q's phanogram meant to convey?"

"I think," he announced, "it means this. Q, who is evidently dead, meant to visualize that fact, meant, so to speak, to deatomize the idea that he was demonetized, and that he wanted two sovereigns tonight."

"And how," I asked, amazed at Annerly's instinctive penetration into the mysteries of the psychic world, "how do you intend to get it to him?"

"I intend," he announced, "to try a bold, a daring experiment, which, if it succeeds, will bring us into immediate connection with the world of spirits. My plan is to leave two sovereigns here upon the edge of the table during the night. If they are gone in the morning, I shall know that Q has contrived to de-astralize himself, and has taken the sovereigns. The only question is, do you happen to have two sovereigns? I myself, unfortunately, have nothing but small change about me."

Here was a piece of rare good fortune, the coincidence of which seemed to add another link to the chain of circumstance. As it happened I had with me the six sovereigns which I had just drawn as my week's pay.

"Luckily," I said, "I am able to arrange that. I happen to have money with me." And I took two sovereigns from my pocket.

Annerly was delighted at our good luck. Our preparations for the experiment were soon made.

We placed the table in the middle of the room in such a way that there could be no fear of contact or collision with any of the furniture. The chairs were carefully set against the wall, and so placed that no two of them occupied the same place as any other two, while the pictures and ornaments about the room were left entirely undisturbed. We were careful not to remove any of the wall-paper from the wall, nor to detach any of the window-panes from the window. When all was ready the two sovereigns were laid side by side upon the table, with the heads up in such a way that the lower sides or tails were supported by only the table itself. We then extinguished the light. I said "Good night" to Annerly, and groped my way out into the dark, feverish with excitement.

My readers may well imagine my state of eagerness to know the result of the experiment. I could scarcely sleep for anxiety to know the issue. I had, of course, every faith in the completeness of our preparations, but was not without misgivings that the experiment might fail, as my own mental temperament and disposition might not be of the precise kind needed for the success of these experiments.

On this score, however, I need have had no alarm. The event showed that my mind was a media, or if the word is better, a transparency, of the very first order for psychic work of this character.

In the morning Annerly came rushing over to my lodgings, his face beaming with excitement.

"Glorious, glorious," he almost shouted, "we have succeeded! The sovereigns are gone. We are in direct monetary communication with Q."

I need not dwell on the exquisite thrill of happiness which went through me. All that day and all the following day, the sense that I was in communication with Q was ever present with me.

My only hope was that an opportunity might offer for the renewal of our inter-communication with the spirit world.

The following night my wishes were gratified. Late in the evening Annerly called me up on the telephone.

"Come over at once to my lodgings," he said. "Q's phanogram is communicating with us."

I hastened over, and arrived almost breathless. "Q has been here again," said Annerly, "and appeared in the same distress as before. A projection of him stood in the room, and kept writing with its finger on the table. I could distinguish the word 'sovereigns,' but nothing more."

"Do you not suppose," I said, "that Q, for some reason which we cannot fathom, wishes us to again leave two sovereigns for him?"

"By Jove!" said Annerly enthusiastically, "I believe you've hit it. At any rate, let us try; we can but fail."

That night we placed again two of my sovereigns on the table, and arranged the furniture with the same scrupulous care as before.

Still somewhat doubtful of my own psychic fitness for the work in which I was engaged, I endeavored to keep my mind so poised as to readily offer a mark for any astral disturbance that might be about. The result showed that it had offered just such a mark. Our experiment succeeded completely. The two coins had vanished in the morning.

For nearly two months we continued our experiments on these lines. At times Annerly himself, so he told me, would leave money, often considerable sums, within reach of the phantasm, which never failed to remove them during the night. But Annerly, being a man of strict honor, never carried on these experiments alone except when it proved impossible to communicate with me in time for me to come.

At other times he would call me up with the simple message, "Q is here," or would send me a telegram, or a written note saying, "Q needs money; bring any that you have, but no more."

On my own part, I was extremely anxious to bring our experiments prominently before the public, or to interest the

Society for Psychic Research, and similar bodies, in the daring transit which we had effected between the world of sentience and the psycho-astrict, or pseudo-ethereal existence. It seemed to me that we alone had succeeded in thus conveying money directly and without mediation, from one world to another. Others, indeed, had done so by the interposition of a medium, or by subscription to an occult magazine, but we had performed the feat with such simplicity that I was anxious to make our experience public, for the benefit of others like myself.

Annerly, however, was averse from this course, being fearful that it might break off our relations with Q.

It was some three months after our first inter-astral psycho-monetary experiment, that there came the culmination of my experiences — so mysterious as to leave me still lost in perplexity.

Annerly had come in to see me one afternoon. He looked nervous and depressed.

"I have just had a psychic communication from Q," he said in answer to my inquiries, "which I can hardly fathom. As far as I can judge, Q has formed some plan for interesting other phantasms in the kind of work that we are doing. He proposes to form, on his side of the gulf, an association that is to work in harmony with us, for monetary dealings on a large scale, between the two worlds."

My reader may well imagine that my eyes almost blazed with excitement at the magnitude of the prospect opened up.

"Q wishes us to gather together all the capital that we can, and to send it across to him, in order that he may be able to organize with him a corporate association of phanograms, or perhaps in this case, one would more correctly call them phantoids."

I had no sooner grasped Annerly's meaning than I became enthusiastic over it.

We decided to try the great experiment that night.

My own worldly capital was, unfortunately, no great amount. I had, however, some £500 in bank stock left to me at my father's decease, which I could, of course, realize within a few hours. I was fearful, however, lest it might prove too small to enable Q to organize his fellow phantoids with it.

I carried the money in notes and sovereigns to Annerly's room, where it was laid on the table. Annerly was fortunately able to contribute a larger sum, which, however, he was not to place beside mine until after I had withdrawn, in order that conjunction of our monetary personalities might not dematerialize the astral phenomenon.

We made our preparations this time with exceptional care, Annerly quietly confident, I, it must be confessed, extremely nervous and fearful of failure. We removed our boots, and walked about on our stockinged feet, and at Annerly's suggestion, not only placed the furniture as before, but turned the coal-scuttle upside down, and laid a wet towel over the top of the wastepaper basket.

All complete, I wrung Annerly's hand, and went out into the darkness.

I waited next morning in vain. Nine o'clock came, ten o'clock, and finally eleven, and still no word of him. Then feverish with anxiety, I sought his lodgings.

Judge of my utter consternation to find that Annerly had disappeared. He had vanished as if off the face of the earth. By what awful error in our preparations, by what neglect of some necessary psychic precautions, he had met his fate, I cannot tell. But the evidence was only too clear, that Annerly had been engulfed into the astral world, carrying with him the money for the transfer of which he had risked his mundane existence.

The proof of his disappearance was easy to find. As soon as I dared do so with discretion I ventured upon a few inquiries. The fact that he had been engulfed while still owing four months' rent for his rooms, and that he had vanished without even having time to pay such bills as he had outstanding with local tradesmen, showed that he must have been devisualized at a moment's notice.

The awful fear that I might be held accountable for his death, prevented me from making the affair public.

Till that moment I had not realized the risks that he had incurred in our reckless dealing with the world of spirits. Annerly fell a victim to the great cause of psychic science, and the record of our experiments remains in the face of prejudice as a witness to its truth.

Moon-Face

JACK LONDON

John Claverhouse was a moon-faced man. You know the kind, cheek-bones wide apart, chin and forehead melting into the cheeks to complete the perfect round, and the nose, broad and pudgy, equidistant from the circumference, flattened against the very center of the face like a dough-ball upon the ceiling. Perhaps that is why I hated him, for truly he had become an offense to my eyes, and I believed the earth to be cumbered with his presence. Perhaps my mother may have been superstitious of the moon and looked upon it over the wrong shoulder at the wrong time.

Be that as it may, I hated John Claverhouse. Not that he had done me what society would consider a wrong or an ill turn. Far from it. The evil was of a deeper, subtler sort; so elusive, so intangible, as to defy clear, definite analysis in words. We all experience such things at some period in our lives. For the first time we see a certain individual, one who the very instant before we did not dream existed; and yet, at the first moment of meeting, we say: "I do not like that man." Why do we not like him? Ah, we do not know why; we know only that we do not. We have taken a dislike, that is all. And so I with John Claverhouse.

What right had such a man to be happy? Yet he was an optimist. He was always gleeful and laughing. All things were always all right, curse him! Ah how it grated on my soul that he should be so happy! Other men could laugh, and it did not bother me. I even used to laugh myself — before I met John Claverhouse.

But his laugh! It irritated me, maddened me, as nothing else under the sun could irritate or madden me. It haunted me, gripped hold of me, and would not let me go. It was a huge, Gargantuan laugh. Waking or sleeping it was always with me, whirring and jarring across my heart-strings like an enormous rasp. At break of day it came whooping across the fields to spoil my pleasant morning revery. Under the aching noonday glare, when the green things drooped and the birds withdrew to the depths of the forest, and all nature drowsed, his great "Ha! ha!" and "Ho! ho!" rose up to the sky and challenged the sun. And at black midnight, from the

lonely crossroads where he turned from town into his own place, came his plaguey cachinnations to rouse me from my sleep and make me writhe and clench my nails into my palms.

I went forth privily in the night-time, and turned his cattle into his fields, and in the morning heard his whooping laugh as he drove them out again. "It is nothing," he said; "the poor, dumb beasties are not to be blamed for straying into fatter pastures."

He had a dog he called "Mars," a big, splendid brute, part deer-hound and part blood-hound, and resembling both. Mars was a great delight to him, and they were always together. But I bided my time, and one day, when opportunity was ripe, lured the animal away and settled for him with strychnine and beefsteak. It made positively no impression on John Claverhouse. His laugh was as hearty and frequent as ever, and his face as much like the full moon as it always had been.

Then I set fire to his haystacks and his barn. But the next morning, being Sunday, he went forth blithe and cheerful.

"Where are you going?" I asked him, as he went by the cross-roads.

"Trout," he said, and his face beamed like a full moon. "I just dote on trout."

Was there ever such an impossible man! His whole harvest had gone up in his haystacks and barn. It was uninsured, I knew. And yet, in the face of famine and the rigorous winter, he went out gayly in quest of a mess of trout, forsooth, because he "doted" on them! Had gloom but rested, no matter how lightly, on his brow, or had his bovine countenance grown long and serious and less like the moon, or had he removed that smile but once from off his face, I am sure I could have forgiven him for existing. But no, he grew only more cheerful under misfortune.

I insulted him. He looked at me in slow and smiling surprise.

"I fight you? Why?" he asked slowly. And then he laughed. "You are so funny! Ho! ho! You'll be the death of me! He! he! he! Oh! Ho! ho! ho!"

What would you? It was past endurance. By the blood of Judas, how I hated him! Then there was that name — Claverhouse! What a name! Wasn't it absurd? Claverhouse! Merciful heaven, WHY Claverhouse? Again and again I asked myself that question. I should not have minded Smith, or Brown, or Jones — but CLAVERHOUSE! I leave it to you. Repeat it to yourself — Claverhouse. Just listen to the ridiculous sound of it — Claverhouse! Should a man live with such a name? I ask of you. "No," you say. And "No" said I.

But I bethought me of his mortgage. What of his crops and barn destroyed, I knew he would be unable to meet it. So I got a shrewd, close-mouthed, tight-fisted money-lender to get the mortgage transferred to him. I did not appear but through this agent I forced the foreclosure, and but few days (no more, believe me, than the law allowed) were given John Claverhouse to remove his goods and chattels from the premises. Then I strolled down to see how he took it, for he had lived there upward of twenty years. But he met me with his saucer-eyes twinkling, and the light glowing and spreading in his face till it was as a full-risen moon.

"Ha! ha! ha!" he laughed. "The funniest tyke, that youngster of mine! Did you ever hear the like? Let me tell you. He was down playing by the edge of the river when a piece of the bank caved in and splashed him. 'O papa!' he cried; 'a great big puddle flewed up and hit me.'"

He stopped and waited for me to join him in his infernal glee.

"I don't see any laugh in it," I said shortly, and I know my face went sour.

He regarded me with wonderment, and then came the damnable light, glowing and spreading, as I have described it, till his face shone soft and warm, like the summer moon, and then the laugh — "Ha! ha! That's funny! You don't see it, eh? He! he! Ho! ho! ho! He doesn't see it! Why, look here. You know a puddle —"

But I turned on my heel and left him. That was the last. I could stand it no longer. The thing must end right there, I thought, curse him! The earth should be quit of him. And as I went over the hill, I could hear his monstrous laugh reverberating against the sky.

Now, I pride myself on doing things neatly, and when I resolved to kill John Claverhouse I had it in mind to do so in such fashion that I should not look back upon it and feel ashamed. I hate bungling, and I hate brutality. To me there is something repugnant in merely striking a man with one's naked fist — faugh! it is sickening! So, to shoot, or stab, or club John Claverhouse (oh, that name!) did not appeal to me. And not only was I impelled to do it neatly and artistically, but also in such manner that not the slightest possible suspicion could be directed against me.

To this end I bent my intellect, and, after a week of profound incubation, I hatched the scheme. Then I set to work. I bought a water spaniel bitch, five months old, and devoted my whole attention to her training. Had anyone spied upon me, they would have remarked that this training consisted entirely of one thing — RETRIEVING. I taught the dog, which I called "Bellona," to fetch sticks I threw into the water, and not only to fetch, but to fetch at once, without mouthing or playing with them. The point was that she was to stop for nothing, but to deliver the stick in all haste. I made a practice of running away and leaving her to chase me, with the stick in her mouth, till she caught me. She was a bright animal, and took to the game with such eagerness that I was soon content.

After that, at the first casual opportunity, I presented Bellona to John Claverhouse. I knew what I was about, for I was aware of a little weakness of his, and of a little private sinning of which he was regularly and inveterately guilty.

"No," he said, when I placed the end of the rope in his hand. "No, you don't mean it." And his mouth opened wide and he grinned all over his damnable moon-face.

"I — I kind of thought, somehow, you didn't like me," he explained. "Wasn't it funny for me to make such a mistake?" And at the thought he held his sides with laughter.

"What is her name?" he managed to ask between paroxysms.

"Bellona," I said.

"He! he!" he tittered. "What a funny name."

I gritted my teeth, for his mirth put them on edge, and snapped out between them, "She was the wife of Mars, you know."

Then the light of the full moon began to suffuse his face, until

he exploded with: "That was my other dog. Well, I guess she's a widow now. Oh! Ho! ho! E! he! he! Ho!" he whooped after me, and I turned and fled swiftly over the hill.

The week passed by, and on Saturday evening I said to him, "You go away Monday, don't you?"

He nodded his head and grinned.

"Then you won't have another chance to get a mess of those trout you just 'dote' on."

But he did not notice the sneer. "Oh, I don't know," he chuckled. "I'm going up tomorrow to try pretty hard."

Thus was assurance made doubly sure, and I went back to my house hugging myself with rapture.

Early next morning I saw him go by with a dip-net and gunnysack, and Bellona trotting at his heels. I knew where he was bound, and cut out by the back pasture and climbed through the

underbrush to the top of the mountain. Keeping carefully out of sight, I followed the crest along for a couple of miles to a natural amphitheater in the hills, where the little river raced down out of a gorge and stopped for breath in a large and placid rock-bound pool. That was the spot! I sat down on the croup of the mountain, where I could see all that occurred, and lighted my pipe.

Ere many minutes had passed, John Claverhouse came plodding up the bed of the stream. Bellona was ambling about him, and they were in high feather, her short, snappy barks mingling with his deeper chest-notes. Arrived at the pool, he threw down the dip-net and sack, and drew from his hip-pocket what looked like a large, fat candle. But I knew it to be a stick of "giant"; for such was his method of catching trout. He dynamited them. He attached the fuse by wrapping the "giant" tightly in a piece of cotton. Then he ignited the fuse and tossed the explosive into the pool.

Like a flash, Bellona was into the pool after it. I could have shrieked aloud for joy. Claverhouse yelled at her, but without avail. He pelted her with clods and rocks, but she swam steadily on till she got the stick of "giant" in her mouth, when she whirled about and headed for shore. Then, for the first time, he realized his danger, and started to run. As foreseen and planned by me, she made the bank and took out after him. Oh, I tell you, it was great! As I have said, the pool lay in a sort of amphitheater. Above and below, the stream could be crossed on stepping-stones. And around and around, up and down and across the stones, raced Claverhouse and Bellona. I could never have believed that such an ungainly man could run so fast. But run he did, Bellona hot-footed after him, and gaining. And then, just as she caught up, he in full stride, and she leaping with nose at his knee, there was a sudden flash, a burst of smoke, a terrific detonation, and where man and dog had been the instant before there was naught to be seen but a big hole in the ground.

"Death from accident while engaged in illegal fishing." That was the verdict of the coroner's jury; and that is why I pride myself on the neat and artistic way in which I finished off John Claverhouse. There was no bungling, no brutality; nothing of which to be ashamed in the whole transaction, as I am sure you will agree. No more does his infernal laugh go echoing among the hills, and no more does his fat moon-face rise up to vex me. My days are peaceful now, and my night's sleep deep.

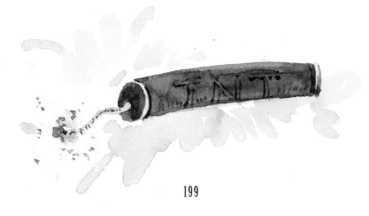

Macbeth

WILLIAM SHAKESPEARE

(excerpt)

ACT IV, SCENE I.
A cavern. In the middle, a boiling cauldron. Thunder.

Enter the three Witches.

First Witch.   Thrice the brinded cat hath mew'd.

Second Witch. Thrice and once the hedge-pig whined.

Third Witch.   Harpier cries, "'Tis time, 'tis time."

First Witch.   Round about the cauldron go;
In the poison'd entrails throw.
Toad, that under cold stone
Days and nights has thirty-one
Swelter'd venom sleeping got,
Boil thou first i' the charmed pot.

All.   Double, double, toil and trouble;
Fire burn and cauldron bubble.

Second Witch.   Fillet of a fenny snake,
              In the cauldron boil and bake;
              Eye of newt and toe of frog,
              Wool of bat and tongue of dog,
              Adder's fork and blind-worm's sting,
              Lizard's leg and howlet's wing,
              For a charm of powerful trouble,
              Like a hell-broth boil and bubble.

All.   Double, double, toil and trouble;
              Fire burn and cauldron bubble.

Third Witch.   Scale of dragon, tooth of wolf,
              Witch's mummy, maw and gulf
              Of the ravin'd salt-sea shark,
              Root of hemlock digg'd i' the dark,
              Liver of blaspheming Jew,
              Gall of goat and slips of yew
              Sliver'd in the moon's eclipse,
              Nose of Turk and Tartar's lips,
              Finger of birth-strangled babe
              Ditch-deliver'd by a drab,
              Make the gruel thick and slab.
              Add thereto a tiger's chaudron,
              For the ingredients of our cauldron.

All.   Double, double, toil and trouble;
              Fire burn and cauldron bubble.

Second Witch.   Cool it with a baboon's blood,
              Then the charm is firm and good.

The Door in the Wall

H.G. WELLS

I.

One confidential evening, not three months ago, Lionel Wallace told me this story of the Door in the Wall. And at the time I thought that so far as he was concerned it was a true story.

He told it me with such a direct simplicity of conviction that I could not do otherwise than believe in him. But in the morning, in my own flat, I woke to a different atmosphere, and as I lay in bed and recalled the things he had told me, stripped of the glamor of his earnest slow voice, denuded of the focused shaded table light, the shadowy atmosphere that wrapped about him, and the pleasant bright things, the dessert and glasses and napery of the dinner we had shared, making them for the time a bright little world quite cut off from everyday realities, I saw it all as frankly incredible. "He was mystifying!" I said, and then: "How well he did it! . . . It isn't quite the thing I should have expected him, of all people, to do well."

Afterwards, as I sat up in bed and sipped my morning tea, I found myself trying to account for the flavor of reality that perplexed me in his impossible reminiscences, by supposing they did in some way suggest, present, convey — I hardly know which word to use — experiences it was otherwise impossible to tell.

Well, I don't resort to that explanation now. I have got over my intervening doubts. I believe now, as I believed at the moment of telling, that Wallace did to the very best of his ability strip the truth of his secret for me. But whether he himself saw, or only thought he saw, whether he himself was the possessor of an inestimable privilege, or the victim of a fantastic dream, I cannot pretend to guess. Even the facts of his death, which ended my doubts forever, throw no light on that. That much the reader must judge for himself.

I forget now what chance comment or criticism of mine moved so reticent a man to confide in me. He was, I think, defending himself against an imputation of slackness and unreliability I had made in relation to a great public movement in which he had disappointed me. But he plunged suddenly. "I have," he said, "a preoccupation —"

"I know," he went on, after a pause that he devoted to the study of his cigar ash, "I have been negligent. The fact is — it isn't a case of ghosts or apparitions — but — it's an odd thing to tell of, Redmond — I am haunted. I am haunted by something — that rather takes the light out of things, that fills me with longings. . . ."

He paused, checked by that English shyness that so often overcomes us when we would speak of moving or grave or beautiful things. "You were at Saint Athelstan's all through," he said, and for a moment that seemed to me quite irrelevant. "Well" — and he paused. Then very haltingly at first, but afterwards more easily, he began to tell of the thing that was hidden in his life, the haunting memory of a beauty and a happiness that filled his heart with insatiable longings that made all the interests and spectacle of worldly life seem dull and tedious and vain to him.

Now that I have the clue to it, the thing seems written visibly in his face. I have a photograph in which that look of detachment has been caught and intensified. It reminds me of what a woman once said of him — a woman who had loved him greatly. "Suddenly," she said, "the interest goes out of him. He forgets you. He doesn't care a rap for you — under his very nose. . . ."

Yet the interest was not always out of him, and when he was holding his attention to a thing Wallace could contrive to be an extremely successful man. His career, indeed, is set with successes. He left me behind him long ago; he soared up over my head, and cut a figure in the world that I couldn't cut — anyhow. He was still a year short of forty, and they say now that he would have been in office and very probably in the new Cabinet if he had lived. At school he always beat me without effort — as it were by nature. We were at school together at Saint Athelstan's College in West Kensington for almost all our school time. He came into the school as my co-equal, but he left far above me, in a blaze of scholarships and brilliant performance. Yet I think I made a fair average running. And it was at school I heard first of the Door in the Wall — that I was to hear of a second time only a month before his death.

To him at least the Door in the Wall was a real door leading through a real wall to immortal realities. Of that I am now quite assured.

And it came into his life early, when he was a little fellow between five and six. I remember how, as he sat making his confession to me with a slow gravity, he reasoned and reckoned the date of it. "There was," he said, "a crimson Virginia creeper in it — all one bright uniform crimson in a clear amber sunshine against a white wall. That came into the impression somehow, though I don't clearly remember how, and there were horse-chestnut leaves upon the clean pavement outside the green door.

205

They were blotched yellow and green, you know, not brown nor dirty, so that they must have been new fallen. I take it that means October. I look out for horse-chestnut leaves every year, and I ought to know.

"If I'm right in that, I was about five years and four months old."

He was, he said, rather a precocious little boy — he learned to talk at an abnormally early age, and he was so sane and "old-fashioned," as people say, that he was permitted an amount of initiative that most children scarcely attain by seven or eight. His mother died when he was born, and he was under the less vigilant and authoritative care of a nursery governess. His father was a stern, preoccupied lawyer, who gave him little attention, and expected great things of him. For all his brightness he found life a little gray and dull I think. And one day he wandered.

He could not recall the particular neglect that enabled him to get away, nor the course he took among the West Kensington roads. All that had faded among the incurable blurs of memory. But the white wall and the green door stood out quite distinctly.

As his memory of that remote childish experience ran, he did at the very first sight of that door experience a peculiar emotion, an attraction, a desire to get to the door and open it and walk in.

And at the same time he had the clearest conviction that either it was unwise or it was wrong of him — he could not tell which — to yield to this attraction. He insisted upon it as a curious thing that he knew from the very beginning — unless memory has played him the queerest trick — that the door was unfastened, and that he could go in as he chose.

I seem to see the figure of that little boy, drawn and repelled. And it was very clear in his mind, too, though why it should be so was never explained, that his father would be very angry if he went through that door.

Wallace described all these moments of hesitation to me with the utmost particularity. He went right past the door, and then, with his hands in his pockets, and making an infantile attempt to whistle, strolled right along beyond the end of the wall. There he recalls a number of mean, dirty shops, and particularly that of a plumber and decorator, with a dusty disorder of earthenware pipes, sheet lead ball taps, pattern books of wall paper, and tins of enamel. He stood pretending to examine these things, and coveting, passionately desiring the green door.

Then, he said, he had a gust of emotion. He made a run for it, lest hesitation should grip him again, he went plump with outstretched hand through the green door and let it slam behind him. And so, in a trice, he came into the garden that has haunted all his life.

It was very difficult for Wallace to give me his full sense of that garden into which he came.

There was something in the very air of it that exhilarated, that gave one a sense of lightness and good happening and well being; there was something in the sight of it that made all its color clean and perfect and subtly luminous. In the instant of coming into it one was exquisitely glad — as only in rare moments and when one is young and joyful one can be glad in this world. And everything was beautiful there. . . .

Wallace mused before he went on telling me. "You see," he said, with the doubtful inflection of a man who pauses at incredible things, "there were two great panthers there . . . Yes, spotted panthers. And I was not afraid. There was a long wide path with marble-edged flower borders on either side, and these two huge velvety beasts were playing there with a ball. One looked up and came towards me, a little curious as it seemed. It came right up to me, rubbed its soft round ear very gently against the small hand I held out and purred. It was, I tell you, an enchanted garden. I know. And the size? Oh! it stretched far and wide, this way and that. I believe there were hills far away. Heaven knows where West Kensington had suddenly got to. And somehow it was just like coming home.

"You know, in the very moment the door swung to behind me, I forgot the road with its fallen chestnut leaves, its cabs and tradesmen's carts, I forgot the sort of gravitational pull back to the discipline and obedience of home, I forgot all hesitations and fear, forgot discretion, forgot all the intimate realities of this life. I became in a moment a very glad and wonder-happy little boy — in another world. It was a world with a different quality, a warmer, more penetrating and mellower light, with a faint clear gladness in its air, and wisps of sun-touched cloud in the blueness of its sky. And before me ran this long wide path, invitingly, with weedless beds on either side, rich with untended flowers, and these two great panthers. I put my little hands fearlessly on their soft fur, and caressed their round ears and the sensitive corners under their ears, and played with them, and it was as though they welcomed me home. There was a keen sense of homecoming in my mind, and when presently a tall, fair girl appeared in the pathway and came to meet me, smiling, and said 'Well?' to me, and lifted me, and kissed me, and put me down, and led me by the hand, there was no amazement, but only an impression of delightful rightness, of being reminded of happy things that had in some strange way been overlooked. There were broad steps, I remember, that came into view between spikes of delphinium, and up these we went to a great avenue between very old and shady dark trees. All down this avenue, you know, between the red chapped stems, were marble seats of honor and statuary, and very tame and friendly white doves. . . .

"And along this avenue my girl-friend led me, looking down — I recall the pleasant lines, the finely-modeled chin of her sweet kind face — asking me questions in a soft, agreeable voice, and telling me things, pleasant things I know, though what they were I was never able to recall . . . And presently a little Capuchin monkey, very clean, with a fur of ruddy brown and kindly hazel eyes, came down a tree to us and ran beside me, looking up at me and grinning, and presently leapt to my shoulder. So we went on our way in great happiness. . . ."

He paused.

"Go on," I said.

"I remember little things. We passed an old man musing among laurels, I remember, and a place gay with paroquets, and came through a broad shaded colonnade to a spacious cool palace, full of pleasant fountains, full of beautiful things, full of the quality and promise of heart's desire. And there were many things

and many people, some that still seem to stand out clearly and some that are a little vague, but all these people were beautiful and kind. In some way — I don't know how — it was conveyed to me that they all were kind to me, glad to have me there, and filling me with gladness by their gestures, by the touch of their hands, by the welcome and love in their eyes. Yes —"

He mused for awhile. "Playmates I found there. That was very much to me, because I was a lonely little boy. They played delightful games in a grass-covered court where there was a sun-dial set about with flowers. And as one played one loved. . . .

"But — it's odd — there's a gap in my memory. I don't remember the games we played. I never remembered. Afterwards, as a child, I spent long hours trying, even with tears, to recall the form of that happiness. I wanted to play it all over again — in my nursery — by myself. No! All I remember is the happiness and two dear playfellows who were most with me. . . . Then presently came a somber dark woman, with a grave, pale face and dreamy eyes, a somber woman wearing a soft long robe of pale purple, who carried a book and beckoned and took me aside with her into a gallery above a hall — though my playmates were loath to have me go, and ceased their game and stood watching as I was carried away. 'Come back to us!' they cried. 'Come back to us soon!' I looked up at her face, but she heeded them not at all. Her face was very gentle and grave. She took me to a seat in the gallery, and I stood beside her, ready to look at her book as she opened it upon her knee. The pages fell open. She pointed, and I looked, marveling, for in the living pages of that book I saw myself; it was a story about myself, and in it were all the things that had happened to me since ever I was born. . . .

"It was wonderful to me, because the pages of that book were not pictures, you understand, but realities."

Wallace paused gravely — looked at me doubtfully.

"Go on," I said. "I understand."

"They were realities — yes, they must have been; people moved and things came and went in them; my dear mother, whom I had near forgotten; then my father, stern and upright, the servants, the nursery, all the familiar things of home. Then the front door and the busy streets, with traffic to and fro: I looked and marveled, and looked half doubtfully again into the woman's face and turned the pages over, skipping this and that, to see more of this book, and more, and so at last I came to myself hovering and hesitating outside the green door in the long white wall, and felt again the conflict and the fear.

"'And next?' I cried, and would have turned on, but the cool hand of the grave woman delayed me.

"'Next?' I insisted, and struggled gently with her hand, pulling up her fingers with all my childish strength, and as she yielded and the page came over she bent down upon me like a shadow and kissed my brow.

"But the page did not show the enchanted garden, nor the panthers, nor the girl who had led me by the hand, nor the playfellows who had been so loth to let me go. It showed a long gray street in West Kensington, on that chill hour of afternoon before the lamps are lit, and I was there, a wretched little figure, weeping aloud, for all that I could do to restrain myself, and I was weeping because I could not return to my dear playfellows who had called after me, 'Come back to us! Come back to us soon!' I was there. This was no page in a book, but harsh reality; that enchanted place and the restraining hand of the grave mother at whose knee I stood had gone — whither have they gone?"

He halted again, and remained for a time, staring into the fire.

"Oh! the wretchedness of that return!" he murmured.

"Well?" I said after a minute or so.

"Poor little wretch I was — brought back to this gray world again! As I realised the fullness of what had happened to me, I gave way to quite ungovernable grief. And the shame and humiliation of that public weeping and my disgraceful homecoming remain with me still. I see again the benevolent-looking old gentleman in gold spectacles who stopped and spoke to me — prodding me first with his umbrella. 'Poor little chap,' said he; 'and are you lost then?' — and me a London boy of five and more! And he must needs bring in a kindly young policeman and make a crowd of me, and so march me home. Sobbing, conspicuous and frightened, I came from the enchanted garden to the steps of my father's house.

"That is as well as I can remember my vision of that garden — the garden that haunts me still. Of course, I can convey nothing of that indescribable quality of translucent unreality, that difference from the common things of experience that hung about it all; but that — that is what happened. If it was a dream, I am sure it was a day-time and altogether extraordinary dream. . . . H'm! — naturally there followed a terrible questioning, by my aunt, my father, the nurse, the governess — everyone. . . .

"I tried to tell them, and my father gave me my first thrashing for telling lies. When afterwards I tried to tell my aunt, she punished me again for my wicked persistence. Then, as I said, everyone was forbidden to listen to me, to hear a word about it. Even my fairy tale books were taken away from me for a time — because I was 'too imaginative.' Eh? Yes, they did that! My father belonged to the old school. . . . And my story was driven back upon myself. I whispered it to my pillow — my pillow that was often damp and salt to my whispering lips with childish tears. And I added always to my official and less fervent prayers this one

heartfelt request: 'Please God I may dream of the garden. Oh! take me back to my garden! Take me back to my garden!'

"I dreamt often of the garden. I may have added to it, I may have changed it; I do not know. . . . All this you understand is an attempt to reconstruct from fragmentary memories a very early experience. Between that and the other consecutive memories of my boyhood there is a gulf. A time came when it seemed impossible I should ever speak of that wonder glimpse again."

I asked an obvious question.

"No," he said. "I don't remember that I ever attempted to find my way back to the garden in those early years. This seems odd to me now, but I think that very probably a closer watch was kept on my movements after this misadventure to prevent my going astray. No, it wasn't until you knew me that I tried for the garden again. And I believe there was a period — incredible as it seems now — when I forgot the garden altogether — when I was about eight or nine it may have been. Do you remember me as a kid at Saint Athelstan's?"

"Rather!"

"I didn't show any signs did I in those days of having a secret dream?"

II.

He looked up with a sudden smile.

"Did you ever play North-West Passage with me? . . . No, of course you didn't come my way!

"It was the sort of game," he went on, "that every imaginative child plays all day. The idea was the discovery of a North-West Passage to school. The way to school was plain enough; the game consisted in finding some way that wasn't plain, starting off ten minutes early in some almost hopeless direction, and working one's way round through unaccustomed streets to my goal. And one day I got entangled among some rather low-class streets on the other side of Campden Hill, and I began to think that for once the game would be against me and that I should get to school late. I tried rather desperately a street that seemed a cul de sac, and found a passage at the end. I hurried through that with renewed hope. 'I shall do it yet,' I said, and passed a row of frowsy little shops that were inexplicably familiar to me, and behold! there was my long white wall and the green door that led to the enchanted garden!

"The thing whacked upon me suddenly. Then, after all, that garden, that wonderful garden, wasn't a dream!". . . .

He paused.

"I suppose my second experience with the green door marks the world of difference there is between the busy life of a schoolboy and the infinite leisure of a child. Anyhow, this second time I didn't for a moment think of going in straight away. You see . . . For one thing my mind was full of the idea of getting to school in time — set on not breaking my record for punctuality. I must surely have felt SOME little desire at least to try the door — yes, I must have felt that. . . . But I seem to remember the attraction of the door mainly as another obstacle to my overmastering determination to get to school. I was immediately interested by this discovery I had made, of course — I went on with my mind full of it — but I went on. It didn't check me. I ran past tugging out my watch, found I had ten minutes still to spare, and then I was going downhill into familiar surroundings. I got to school, breathless, it is true, and wet with perspiration, but in time. I can remember hanging up my coat and hat . . . Went right by it and left it behind me. Odd, eh?"

He looked at me thoughtfully. "Of course, I didn't know then that it wouldn't always be there. School boys have limited imaginations. I suppose I thought it was an awfully jolly thing to have it there, to know my way back to it, but there was the school tugging at me. I expect I was a good deal distraught and inattentive that morning, recalling what I could of the beautiful strange people I should presently see again. Oddly enough I had no doubt in my mind that they would be glad to see me . . . Yes, I must have thought of the garden that morning just as a jolly sort of place to which one might resort in the interludes of a strenuous scholastic career.

"I didn't go that day at all. The next day was a half holiday, and that may have weighed with me. Perhaps, too, my state of inattention brought down impositions upon me and docked the margin of time necessary for the detour. I don't know. What I do know is that in the meantime the enchanted garden was so much upon my mind that I could not keep it to myself.

"I told — What was his name? — a ferrety-looking youngster we used to call Squiff."

"Young Hopkins," said I.

"Hopkins it was. I did not like telling him, I had a feeling that in some way it was against the rules to tell him, but I did. He was walking part of the way home with me; he was talkative, and if we had not talked about the enchanted garden we should have talked of something else, and it was intolerable to me to think about any other subject. So I blabbed.

"Well, he told my secret. The next day in the play interval I found myself surrounded by half a dozen bigger boys, half teasing and wholly curious to hear more of the enchanted garden. There was that big Fawcett — you remember him? — and Carnaby and Morley Reynolds. You weren't there by any chance? No, I think I should have remembered if you were. . . .

"A boy is a creature of odd feelings. I was, I really believe, in

spite of my secret self-disgust, a little flattered to have the attention of these big fellows. I remember particularly a moment of pleasure caused by the praise of Crawshaw — you remember Crawshaw major, the son of Crawshaw the composer? — who said it was the best lie he had ever heard. But at the same time there was a really painful undertow of shame at telling what I felt was indeed a sacred secret. That beast Fawcett made a joke about the girl in green —"

Wallace's voice sank with the keen memory of that shame. "I pretended not to hear," he said. "Well, then Carnaby suddenly called me a young liar and disputed with me when I said the thing was true. I said I knew where to find the green door, could lead them all there in ten minutes. Carnaby became outrageously virtuous, and said I'd have to — and bear out my words or suffer. Did you ever have Carnaby twist your arm? Then perhaps you'll understand how it went with me. I swore my story was true. There was nobody in the school then to save a chap from Carnaby though Crawshaw put in a word or so. Carnaby had got his game. I grew excited and red-eared, and a little frightened, I behaved altogether like a silly little chap, and the outcome of it all was that instead of starting alone for my enchanted garden, I led the way presently — cheeks flushed, ears hot, eyes smarting, and my soul one burning misery and shame — for a party of six mocking, curious and threatening school-fellows.

"We never found the white wall and the green door. . . ."

"You mean? —"

"I mean I couldn't find it. I would have found it if I could.

"And afterwards when I could go alone I couldn't find it. I never found it. I seem now to have been always looking for it through my school-boy days, but I've never come upon it again."

"Did the fellows — make it disagreeable?"

"Beastly. . . . Carnaby held a council over me for wanton lying. I remember how I sneaked home and upstairs to hide the marks of my blubbering. But when I cried myself to sleep at last it wasn't for Carnaby, but for the garden, for the beautiful afternoon I had hoped for, for the sweet friendly women and the waiting playfellows and the game I had hoped to learn again, that beautiful forgotten game. . . .

"I believed firmly that if I had not told — . . . I had bad times after that — crying at night and woolgathering by day. For two terms I slackened and had bad reports. Do you remember? Of course you would! It was YOU — your beating me in mathematics that brought me back to the grind again."

III.

For a time my friend stared silently into the red heart of the fire. Then he said: "I never saw it again until I was seventeen.

"It leapt upon me for the third time — as I was driving to Paddington on my way to Oxford and a scholarship. I had just one momentary glimpse. I was leaning over the apron of my hansom smoking a cigarette, and no doubt thinking myself no end of a man of the world, and suddenly there was the door, the wall, the dear sense of unforgettable and still attainable things.

"We clattered by — I too taken by surprise to stop my cab until we were well past and round a corner. Then I had a queer moment, a double and divergent movement of my will: I tapped the little door in the roof of the cab, and brought my arm down to pull out my watch. 'Yes, sir!' said the cabman, smartly. 'Er — well — it's nothing,' I cried. 'MY mistake! We haven't much time! Go on!' and he went on. . . .

"I got my scholarship. And the night after I was told of that I sat over my fire in my little upper room, my study, in my father's house, with his praise — his rare praise — and his sound counsels ringing in my ears, and I smoked my favorite pipe — the formidable bulldog of adolescence — and thought of that door in the long white wall. 'If I had stopped,' I thought, 'I should have missed my scholarship, I should have missed Oxford — muddled all the fine career before me! I begin to see things better!' I fell musing deeply, but I did not doubt then this career of mine was a thing that merited sacrifice.

"Those dear friends and that clear atmosphere seemed very sweet to me, very fine, but remote. My grip was fixing now upon the world. I saw another door opening — the door of my career."

He stared again into the fire. Its red lights picked out a stubborn strength in his face for just one flickering moment, and then it vanished again.

"Well", he said and sighed, "I have served that career. I have done — much work, much hard work. But I have dreamt of the enchanted garden a thousand dreams, and seen its door, or at least glimpsed its door, four times since then. Yes — four times. For a while this world was so bright and interesting, seemed so full of meaning and opportunity that the half-effaced charm of the garden was by comparison gentle and remote. Who wants to pat panthers on the way to dinner with pretty women and distinguished men? I came down to London from Oxford, a man of bold promise that I have done something to redeem. Something — and yet there have been disappointments. . . .

"Twice I have been in love — I will not dwell on that — but once, as I went to someone who, I know, doubted whether I dared to come, I took a short cut at a venture through an unfrequented road near Earl's Court, and so happened on a white wall and a familiar green door. 'Odd!' said I to myself, 'but I thought this place was on Campden Hill. It's the place I never could find somehow — like counting Stonehenge — the place of that queer day dream of mine.' And I went by it intent upon my purpose. It had no appeal to me that afternoon.

"I had just a moment's impulse to try the door, three steps aside were needed at the most — though I was sure enough in my heart that it would open to me — and then I thought that doing so might delay me on the way to that appointment in which I thought my honor was involved. Afterwards I was sorry for my punctuality — I might at least have peeped in I thought, and waved a hand to those panthers, but I knew enough by this time not to seek again belatedly that which is not found by seeking. Yes, that time made me very sorry. . . .

"Years of hard work after that and never a sight of the door. It's only recently it has come back to me. With it there has come a sense as though some thin tarnish had spread itself over my world. I began to think of it as a sorrowful and bitter thing that I should never see that door again. Perhaps I was suffering a little from overwork — perhaps it was what I've heard spoken of as the feeling of forty. I don't know. But certainly the keen brightness that makes effort easy has gone out of things recently, and that just at a time with all these new political developments — when I ought to be working. Odd, isn't it? But I do begin to find life toilsome, its rewards, as I come near them, cheap. I began a little while ago to want the garden quite badly. Yes — and I've seen it three times."

"The garden?"

"No — the door! And I haven't gone in!"

He leaned over the table to me, with an enormous sorrow in his voice as he spoke. "Thrice I have had my chance — THRICE! If ever that door offers itself to me again, I swore, I will go in out of this dust and heat, out of this dry glitter of vanity, out of these toilsome futilities. I will go and never return. This time I will stay. . . . I swore it and when the time came — I DIDN'T GO.

"Three times in one year have I passed that door and failed to enter. Three times in the last year.

"The first time was on the night of the snatch division on the Tenants' Redemption Bill, on which the Government was saved by a majority of three. You remember? No one on our side — perhaps very few on the opposite side — expected the end that night. Then the debate collapsed like eggshells. I and Hotchkiss were dining with his cousin at Brentford, we were both unpaired, and we were called up by telephone, and set off at once in his cousin's motor. We got in barely in time, and on the way we passed my wall and door — livid in the moonlight, blotched with hot yellow as the glare of our lamps lit it, but unmistakable. 'My God!' cried I. 'What?' said Hotchkiss. 'Nothing!' I answered, and the moment passed.

"'I've made a great sacrifice,' I told the whip as I got in. 'They all have,' he said, and hurried by.

"I do not see how I could have done otherwise then. And the next occasion was as I rushed to my father's bedside to bid that stern old man farewell. Then, too, the claims of life were imperative. But the third time was different; it happened a week ago. It fills me with hot remorse to recall it. I was with Gurker and Ralphs — it's no secret now you know that I've had my talk with Gurker. We had been dining at Frobisher's, and the talk had become intimate between us. The question of my place in the reconstructed ministry lay always just over the boundary of the

discussion. Yes — yes. That's all settled. It needn't be talked about yet, but there's no reason to keep a secret from you.... Yes — thanks! thanks! But let me tell you my story.

"Then, on that night things were very much in the air. My position was a very delicate one. I was keenly anxious to get some definite word from Gurker, but was hampered by Ralphs' presence. I was using the best power of my brain to keep that light and careless talk not too obviously directed to the point that concerns me. I had to. Ralphs' behavior since has more than justified my caution.... Ralphs, I knew, would leave us beyond the Kensington High Street, and then I could surprise Gurker by a sudden frankness. One has sometimes to resort to these little devices.... And then it was that in the margin of my field of vision I became aware once more of the white wall, the green door before us down the road.

"We passed it talking. I passed it. I can still see the shadow of Gurker's marked profile, his opera hat tilted forward over his prominent nose, the many folds of his neck wrap going before my shadow and Ralphs' as we sauntered past.

"I passed within twenty inches of the door. 'If I say good-night to them, and go in,' I asked myself, 'what will happen?' And I was all a-tingle for that word with Gurker.

"I could not answer that question in the tangle of my other problems. 'They will think me mad,' I thought. 'And suppose I vanish now!—Amazing disappearance of a prominent politician!' That weighed with me. A thousand inconceivably petty worldlinesses weighed with me in that crisis."

Then he turned on me with a sorrowful smile, and, speaking slowly; "Here I am!" he said.

"Here I am!" he repeated, "and my chance has gone from me. Three times in one year the door has been offered me — the door that goes into peace, into delight, into a beauty beyond dreaming, a kindness no man on earth can know. And I have rejected it, Redmond, and it has gone —"

"How do you know?"

"I know. I know. I am left now to work it out, to stick to the tasks that held me so strongly when my moments came. You say, I have success — this vulgar, tawdry, irksome, envied thing. I have it." He had a walnut in his big hand. "If that was my success," he said, and crushed it, and held it out for me to see.

"Let me tell you something, Redmond. This loss is destroying me. For two months, for ten weeks nearly now, I have done no work at all, except the most necessary and urgent duties. My soul is full of inappeasable regrets. At nights — when it is less likely I shall be recognized — I go out. I wander. Yes. I wonder what people would think of that if they knew. A Cabinet Minister, the responsible head of that most vital of all departments, wandering alone — grieving — sometimes near audibly lamenting — for a door, for a garden!"

IV.

I can see now his rather pallid face, and the unfamiliar somber fire that had come into his eyes. I see him very vividly tonight. I sit recalling his words, his tones, and last evening's Westminster Gazette still lies on my sofa, containing the notice of his death. At lunch today the club was busy with him and the strange riddle of his fate.

They found his body very early yesterday morning in a deep excavation near East Kensington Station. It is one of two shafts that have been made in connection with an extension of the railway southward. It is protected from the intrusion of the public by a hoarding upon the high road, in which a small doorway has been cut for the convenience of some of the workmen who live in that direction. The doorway was left unfastened through a misunderstanding between two gangers, and through it he made his way. . . .

My mind is darkened with questions and riddles.

It would seem he walked all the way from the House that night — he has frequently walked home during the past Session — and so it is I figure his dark form coming along the late and empty streets, wrapped up, intent. And then did the pale electric lights near the station cheat the rough planking into a semblance of white? Did that fatal unfastened door awaken some memory?

Was there, after all, ever any green door in the wall at all?

I do not know. I have told his story as he told it to me. There are times when I believe that Wallace was no more than the victim of the coincidence between a rare but not unprecedented type of hallucination and a careless trap, but that indeed is not my profoundest belief. You may think me superstitious if you will, and foolish; but, indeed, I am more than half convinced that he had in truth, an abnormal gift, and a sense, something — I know not what — that in the guise of wall and door offered him an outlet, a secret and peculiar passage of escape into another and altogether more beautiful world. At any rate, you will say, it betrayed him in the end. But did it betray him? There you touch the inmost mystery of these dreamers, these men of vision and the imagination.

We see our world fair and common, the hoarding and the pit. By our daylight standard he walked out of security into darkness, danger and death. But did he see like that?

An Unposted Letter

NEWTON MACTAVISH

Outside, a hammer pounded mockingly; the gallows were under construction. Through the iron bars of the prison window shone a few straggling shafts of sunlight. My client rested on his elbows, his chin in his hands. The light glistened on his matted hair. He heard the hammering outside.

"I guess I may's well write a line to Bill," he said, not raising his head. "Kin you get a pencil and paper?"

I got them, and then waited until he had written:

"Dear Bill, — By the sound of things, I reckon I've got to swing this trip. I've had a hope all along that they might git scent on the right track; but I see that Six-Eye'll be 'bliged to kick the bucket, with head up — the galleys is goin' up mighty fast.

"I say, Bill, there ain't no good in burglarin'. I swore once I'd quit it, and wish I had. But a feller can't allus do just as he fancies; I guess he can't allus do it, kin he, Bill? You never knew how I got into this scrape, did you?

"One day I was standin' around, just standin' around, nothin' doin', when I saw a pair of runaway horses a-comin' down the street like mad. I jumped out and caught the nigh one by the bridle. I hauled 'em up mighty sudden, but somethin' swung me

round, and I struck my head agin the neck-yoke, kersmash.

"When I come to, I was sittin' back in the carriage with the sweetest faced girl bendin' over me, and wipin' my face with cool water. She asked where she would drive me home; and, do you know, Bill, for the first time, I was ashamed to say where. But I told her, and, so help me, she came clear down in there with me, and made Emily put me to bed. She left money, and every day till I got well she come out and sat and read the Bible and all them things. Do you know, Bill, it wasn't long afore things seemed different. I couldn't look at her pure, sweet face and plan a job. The last day she came I made up my mind I'd try somethin' else — quit burglarin'.

"I started out to get work. One man asked me what I'd served my time at. I said I'd served most of it in jail, and then he wouldn't have anythin' to do with me. A chap gave me a couple of days breakin' stones in a cellar. He said I did it so good he guessed I

must have been in jail. After that I couldn't get nothin' to do, because no one wouldn't have nothin' to do with a jail-bird, and I had made up my mind to tell the truth.

"At last Emily began to kick and little Bob to cry for grub. I got sick of huntin' for work, and it seemed as if everybody was pushin' me back to my old job. I got disgusted. I had to do somethin', so I sat down and planned to do a big house in the suburbs. I'd sized it up before.

"The moon was high that night, so I waited till it went down, long after midnight. I found the back door already open, so it was a snap to git in.

"I went upstairs and picked on a side room near the front. I eased the door and looked in. A candle flickered low, and flames danced from a few coals in the fireplace.

"I entered noiselessly.

"A high-backed chair was in front of the hearth. I sneaked up and looked over the top. A young girl, all dressed in white, laid there asleep. Her hair hung over her shoulders; she looked like as if she'd come home from a dance, and just threw herself there tired out.

"Just as I was goin' to turn away, the flames in the fireplace flickered, and I caught the glow of rubies at the girl's throat. How they shone and gleamed and shot fire from their blood-red depths! The candle burned low and sputtered; but the coals on the hearth flickered, the rubies glowed, and the girl breathed soft in her sleep.

"'It's an easy trick,' I said to myself, and I leaned over the back of the chair, my breath fanning the light hair that fell over her shoulders. I took out my knife and reached over. Just then the fire burned up a bit. As I leaned over I saw her sweet, girlish face, and, so h'lp me, Bill, it was her, her whose face I couldn't look into and plan a job.

"Hardly knowing it, I bared my head, and stood there knife in hand, the blood rushin' to my face, and my feelin's someway seemin' to go agin me.

"I looked at her, and gradually closed my knife and straightened up from that sneakin' shape a feller gets into. I remembered a verse that she used to read to me, 'Ye shall not go forth empty-handed,' so I said to myself I'd try again. But just as I was turning to go, I heard a shot in the next room; then a heavy thud. I stood stock-still for a jiffy, and then ran out in time to see someone dart down the stairs. At the bottom I heard a stumble. I hurried along the hall and ran straight into the arms of the butler.

"I guess someone else was doin' that job that night. But they had me slicker'n a whistle. 'Twas no use; everythin' went agin me.

I had on my big revolver, the mate to the one you got. As it happened, one chamber was empty, and the ball they took from the old man's head was the same size. I had a bad record; it was all up with me. The only thing they brought up in court to the contrary was the top of an ear they found in the hall, where someone must have hit agin somethin' sharp. But they wouldn't listen to my lawyer.

"Give up burglarin,' Bill; see what I've come to. But I hope you'll do a turn for Emily if ever she's in need, and don't learn little Bob filchin.' Do this for an old pal's sake, Bill."

The doomed man stopped writing, as the last shaft of sunlight passed beyond the iron bars of the prison window. Outside the hammering had ceased; the scaffold was finished.

"You'll find Emily, my wife, in the back room of the basement at 126, River Street," said my client, handing me the letter. "She'll tell you where to find Bill."

I took the letter, but did not then know its contents. I started, but he called me back.

"You have a flower in your button-hole," he said. "I'd like to wrap it up and send it to Emily."

Next day, after the sentence of the law had been executed, I went to find Emily. I descended the musty old staircase at 126 River Street, where all was filth and squalor. At the back room I stopped and rapped. A towzy head was thrust out of the next door.

"They're gone," it said.

"Where?"

"Don't know. The woman went with some man."

"Did you know him?"

"I saw him here before sometimes, but the top of his ear wasn't cut off then. They called him Bill — sort of pal."

"And where's the little boy?"

"He's gone to the Shelter."

I went out into the pure air, and, standing on the kerbstone, read the letter:

". . . The only thing they brought up in court to the contrary was the top of an ear. . . ."

When I had finished, I remembered the flower in my hand. I didn't throw it away; I took it to my office and have it there still, wrapped in the paper as he gave it to me.

The Thing and I

SEAN O'HUIGIN

i heard
a great
howling
a screeching
and yowling
as i woke
on a
dark moonless
night
the windows
were shaking
the house
it was
quaking
i reached
out to
turn on
the light
my hand
it touched

something
that set
my heart
thumping
a substance
all sticky
and warm
it felt like
raw liver
it set me

aquiver
and then
it crawled
all up
my arm
my face
was soon
covered
i thought
i'd be
smothered
i tried to
let out
a loud
scream
"oh please"
i thought
"mother
let me
discover
this whole
thing is
only a
dream"
i rose from
the bed
the "thing"
'round my
head
i struggled
to find

the light
switch
when there
by the mirror
i heard very
clear
a laugh

AHAHAH EHEHEHEH HAHAHAHAHA AAA

that must
come from
a witch
my body
was dripping
my feet
started
slipping
the "thing"
had encased
me in slime
and now
i have come
to your
house my
dear one
and soon
you shall
be
one of
mine

Beginning with the Ears

ARIELLE NORTH OLSON
and HOWARD SCHWARTZ

There once was a man named Abdu who had trouble finding work. He was very poor, and his wife and children were always hungry.

In desperation, Abdu left the town where he lived to see if he could earn a few coins in the countryside. But no matter how far he walked, he found no one who needed his help. By afternoon, he was weak and tired, for he had not had a bite to eat all day.

Suddenly he saw an old woman coming toward him. She was bent and wrinkled and wore a flowered kerchief over her hair. "Where are you going?" she asked.

"Who knows," he cried. "I must wander from place to place until I earn enough to support my wife and children."

"Do not despair," she said. "Bring your family to live with me, Abdu, and we will share my wealth."

Abdu was amazed. "Who are you?" he asked. "And how do you know my name?"

"I'm your cousin," she replied. "I'm old and alone and would like your company. If you and your family live with me, no one will have to go hungry."

Abdu could hardly believe his ears, and hope began to grow in his heart. He felt strong again, and he ran home to tell his wife and children all that he had heard. They were delighted to learn of their long-lost cousin.

That very evening they left town and walked out to meet the old woman, who was waiting for them in the middle of the road.

She took them home and let them eat to their hearts' content. "And soon you shall have milk to drink," she told them. She picked up a pail and went out to the barn.

Abdu's wife followed to see if she could help with the milking, but as she approached the barn, she overheard the old woman talking to her cow. "Tomorrow I shall eat my guests," she said.

The cow mooed as if to say, "No, no, no!" And Abdu's wife rushed back to the house to warn her husband.

"We must leave at once," she cried. "The old woman told the cow she is planning to eat us tomorrow!"

Abdu was angry. "You didn't hear right," he said. "Look how kind and generous she has been."

Abdu's wife finally agreed to stay, but she was too frightened to sleep all night.

The next morning, Abdu's wife again followed the old woman out to the barn. Again she overheard what the old woman said. "Ah, today I shall eat my guests!" And again the cow mooed as if to say, "No, no, no!"

Abdu's wife ran back to the house as fast as she could. "We can't stay here a moment longer. The old woman is planning to eat us today!" she cried. But still Abdu refused to listen.

"Is there something wrong with your ears?" she shouted. "Stay if you like, but I am taking the children back home." And that is exactly what she did.

When the old woman returned from the barn and saw that only Abdu was left, she decided to eat him right away. She blocked the doorway and screeched at him, "I'm not your cousin!" Her back straightened, her wrinkles faded away, and her kerchief fell off, revealing long, dark hair. "I am a witch," she said, "who likes nothing better than eating the fools who come to live in my house!

"Tell me," she asked, "which part of your body should I eat first?" She pulled a metal file from her pocket and began to sharpen her teeth.

Abdu was trembling from head to toe. He realized he was trapped and there was nothing he could do.

"My wife warned me," he said, "but I would not listen. So begin with my ears."

The Toll-House

W.W. JACOBS

"It's all nonsense," said Jack Barnes. "Of course people have died in the house; people die in every house. As for the noises — wind in the chimney and rats in the wainscot are very convincing to a nervous man. Give me another cup of tea, Meagle."

"Lester and White are first," said Meagle, who was presiding at the tea-table of the Three Feathers Inn. "You've had two."

Lester and White finished their cups with irritating slowness, pausing between sips to sniff the aroma, and to discover the sex and dates of arrival of the "strangers" which floated in some numbers in the beverage. Mr. Meagle served them to the brim, and then, turning to the grimly expectant Mr. Barnes, blandly requested him to ring for hot water.

"We'll try and keep your nerves in their present healthy condition," he remarked. "For my part I have a sort of half-and-half belief in the supernatural."

"All sensible people have," said Lester. "An aunt of mine saw a ghost once."

White nodded.

"I had an uncle that saw one," he said.

"It always is somebody else that sees them," said Barnes.

"Well, there is the house," said Meagle, "a large house at an absurdly low rent, and nobody will take it. It has taken toll of at least one life of every family that has lived there — however short the time — and since it has stood empty caretaker after caretaker has died there. The last caretaker died fifteen years ago."

"Exactly," said Barnes. "Long enough ago for legends to accumulate."

"I'll bet you a sovereign you won't spend the night there alone, for all your talk," said White suddenly.

"And I," said Lester.

"No," said Barnes slowly. "I don't believe in ghosts nor in any supernatural things whatever; all the same, I admit that I should not care to pass a night there alone."

"But why not?" inquired White.

"Wind in the chimney," said Meagle, with a grin.

"Rats in the wainscot," chimed in Lester.

"As you like," said Barnes, colouring.

"Suppose we all go?" said Meagle. "Start after supper, and get there about eleven? We have been walking for ten days now without an adventure — except Barnes's discovery that ditch-water smells longest. It will be a novelty, at any rate, and, if we break the spell by all surviving, the grateful owner ought to come down handsome."

"Let's see what the landlord has to say about it first," said Lester. "There is no fun in passing a night in an ordinary empty house. Let us make sure that it is haunted."

He rang the bell, and, sending for the landlord, appealed to him in the name of our common humanity not to let them waste a night watching in a house in which specters and hobgoblins had no part. The reply was more than reassuring, and the landlord, after describing with considerable art the exact appearance of a head which had been seen hanging out of a window in the moonlight, wound up with a polite but urgent request that they would settle his bill before they went.

"It's all very well for you young gentlemen to have your fun," he said indulgently; "but, supposing as how you are all found dead in the morning, what about me? It ain't called the Toll-House for nothing, you know."

"Who died there last?" inquired Barnes, with an air of polite derision.

"A tramp," was the reply. "He went there for the sake of half-a-crown, and they found him next morning hanging from the balusters, dead."

"Suicide," said Barnes. "Unsound mind."

The landlord nodded. "That's what the jury brought it in," he said slowly; "but his mind was sound enough when he went in there. I'd known him, off and on, for years. I'm a poor man, but I wouldn't spend the night in that house for a hundred pounds."

He repeated this remark as they started on their expedition a few hours later. They left as the inn was closing for the night; bolts shot noisily behind them, and, as the regular customers trudged slowly homewards, they set off at a brisk pace in the direction of the house. Most of the cottages were already in darkness, and lights in others went out as they passed.

"It seems rather hard that we have got to lose a night's rest in order to convince Barnes of the existence of ghosts," said White.

"It's in a good cause," said Meagle. "A most worthy object; and something seems to tell me that we shall succeed. You didn't forget the candles, Lester?"

"I have brought two," was the reply; "all the old man could spare."

There was but little moon, and the night was cloudy. The road between high hedges was dark, and in one place, where it ran

through a wood, so black that they twice stumbled in the uneven ground at the side of it.

"Fancy leaving our comfortable beds for this!" said White again. "Let me see; this desirable residential sepulchre lies to the right, doesn't it?"

"Farther on," said Meagle.

They walked on for some time in silence, broken only by White's tribute to the softness, the cleanliness, and the comfort of the bed which was receding farther and farther into the distance. Under Meagle's guidance they turned off at last to the right, and, after a walk of a quarter of a mile, saw the gates of the house before them.

The lodge was almost hidden by overgrown shrubs and the drive was choked with rank growths. Meagle leading, they pushed through it until the dark pile of the house loomed above them.

"There is a window at the back where we can get in, so the landlord says," said Lester, as they stood before the hall door.

"Window?" said Meagle. "Nonsense. Let's do the thing properly. Where's the knocker?"

He felt for it in the darkness and gave a thundering rat-tat-tat at the door.

"Don't play the fool," said Barnes crossly.

"Ghostly servants are all asleep," said Meagle gravely, "but *I'll* wake them up before I've done with them. It's scandalous keeping us out here in the dark."

He plied the knocker again, and the noise volleyed in the emptiness beyond. Then with a sudden exclamation he put out his hands and stumbled forward.

"Why, it was open all the time," he said, with an odd catch in his voice. "Come on."

"I don't believe it was open," said Lester, hanging back. "Somebody is playing us a trick."

"Nonsense," said Meagle sharply. "Give me a candle. Thanks. Who's got a match?"

Barnes produced a box and struck one, and Meagle, shielding the candle with his hand, led the way forward to the foot of the stairs. "Shut the door, somebody," he said; "there's too much draft."

"It is shut," said White, glancing behind him.

Meagle fingered his chin. "Who shut it?" he inquired, looking from one to the other. "Who came in last?"

"I did," said Lester, "but I don't remember shutting it — perhaps I did, though."

Meagle, about to speak, thought better of it, and, still carefully guarding the flame, began to explore the house, with the others close behind. Shadows danced on the walls and lurked in the corners as they proceeded. At the end of the passage they found a second staircase, and ascending it slowly gained the first floor.

"Careful!" said Meagle, as they gained the landing.

He held the candle forward and showed where the balusters had broken away. Then he peered curiously into the void beneath.

"This is where the tramp hanged himself, I suppose," he said thoughtfully.

"You've got an unwholesome mind," said White, as they walked on. "This place is quite creepy enough without you remembering that. Now let's find a comfortable room and have a little nip of whisky apiece and a pipe. How will this do?"

He opened a door at the end of the passage and revealed a small square room. Meagle led the way with the candle, and, first melting a drop or two of tallow, stuck it on the mantelpiece. The others seated themselves on the floor and watched pleasantly as White drew from his pocket a small bottle of whisky and a tin cup.

"H'm! I've forgotten the water," he exclaimed.

"I'll soon get some," said Meagle.

He tugged violently at the bell-handle, and the rusty jangling of a bell sounded from a distant kitchen. He rang again.

"Don't play the fool," said Barnes roughly.

Meagle laughed. "I only wanted to convince you," he said kindly. "There ought to be, at any rate, one ghost in the servants' hall."

Barnes held up his hand for silence.

"Yes?" said Meagle, with a grin at the other two. "Is anybody coming?"

"Suppose we drop this game and go back," said Barnes suddenly. "I don't believe in spirits, but nerves are outside anybody's command. You may laugh as you like, but it really seemed to me that I heard a door open below and steps on the stairs."

His voice was drowned in a roar of laughter.

"He is coming round," said Meagle, with a smirk. "By the time I have done with him he will be a confirmed believer. Well, who will go and get some water? Will, you, Barnes?"

"No," was the reply.

"If there is any it might not be safe to drink after all these years," said Lester. "We must do without it."

Meagle nodded, and taking a seat on the floor held out his hand for the cup. Pipes were lit, and the clean, wholesome smell of tobacco filled the room. White produced a pack of cards; talk and laughter rang through the room and died away reluctantly in distant corridors.

"Empty rooms always delude me into the belief that I possess a deep voice," said Meagle. "Tomorrow I ——"

He started up with a smothered exclamation as the light went

out suddenly and something struck him on the head. The others sprang to their feet. Then Meagle laughed.

"It's the candle," he exclaimed. "I didn't stick it enough."

Barnes struck a match, and re-lighting the candle, stuck it on the mantelpiece, and sitting down took up his cards again.

"What was I going to say?" said Meagle. "Oh, I know; to-morrow I ——"

"Listen!" said White, laying his hand on the other's sleeve. "Upon my word I really thought I heard a laugh."

"Look here!" said Barnes. "What do you say to going back? I've had enough of this. I keep fancying that I hear things too; sounds of something moving about in the passage outside. I know it's only fancy, but it's uncomfortable."

"You go if you want to," said Meagle, "and we will play dummy. Or you might ask the tramp to take your hand for you, as you go downstairs."

Barnes shivered and exclaimed angrily. He got up, and, walking to the half-closed door, listened.

"Go outside," said Meagle, winking at the other two. "I'll dare you to go down to the hall door and back by yourself."

Barnes came back, and, bending forward, lit his pipe at the candle.

"I am nervous, but rational," he said, blowing out a thin cloud of smoke. "My nerves tell me that there is something prowling up and down the long passage outside; my reason tells me that that is all nonsense. Where are my cards?"

He sat down again, and, taking up his hand, looked through it carefully and led.

"Your play, White," he said, after a pause.

White made no sign.

"Why, he is asleep," said Meagle. "Wake up, old man. Wake up and play."

Lester, who was sitting next to him, took the sleeping man by the arm and shook him, gently at first and then with some roughness but White, with his back against the wall and his head bowed, made no sign. Meagle bawled in his ear, and then turned a puzzled face to the others.

"He sleeps like the dead," he said, grimacing. "Well, there are still three of us to keep each other company."

"Yes," said Lester, nodding. "Unless — Good Lord! suppose ——"

He broke off, and eyed them, trembling.

"Suppose what?" inquired Meagle.

"Nothing," stammered Lester. "Let's wake him. Try him again. *White!* WHITE!"

"It's no good," said Meagle seriously; "there's something wrong about that sleep."

"That's what I meant," said Lester; "and if *he* goes to sleep like that, why shouldn't ——"

Meagle sprang to his feet. "Nonsense," he said roughly. "He's tired out; that's all. Still, let's take him up and clear out. You take his legs and Barnes will lead the way with the candle. *Yes? Who's that?*"

He looked up quickly towards the door. "Thought I heard somebody tap," he said, with a shamefaced laugh. "Now, Lester, up with him. One, two — *Lester! Lester!*"

He sprang forward too late; Lester, with his face buried in his arms, had rolled over on the floor fast asleep, and his utmost efforts failed to awake him.

"He — is — asleep," he stammered. "Asleep!"

Barnes, who had taken the candle from the mantelpiece, stood peering at the sleepers in silence and dropping tallow over the floor.

"We must get out of this," said Meagle. "Quick!"

Barnes hesitated. "We can't leave them here —" he began.

"We must," said Meagle, in strident tones. "If you go to sleep I shall go — Quick! Come!"

He seized the other by the arm and strove to drag him to the door. Barnes shook him off, and, putting the candle back on the mantelpiece, tried again to arouse the sleepers.

"It's no good," he said at last, and, turning from them, watched Meagle. "Don't you go to sleep," he said anxiously.

Meagle shook his head, and they stood for some time in uneasy silence. "May as well shut the door," said Barnes at last.

He crossed over and closed it gently. Then at a scuffling noise behind him he turned and saw Meagle in a heap on the hearthstone.

With a sharp catch in his breath he stood motionless. Inside the room the candle, fluttering in the draught, showed dimly the grotesque attitudes of the sleepers. Beyond the door there seemed to his overwrought imagination a strange and stealthy

256

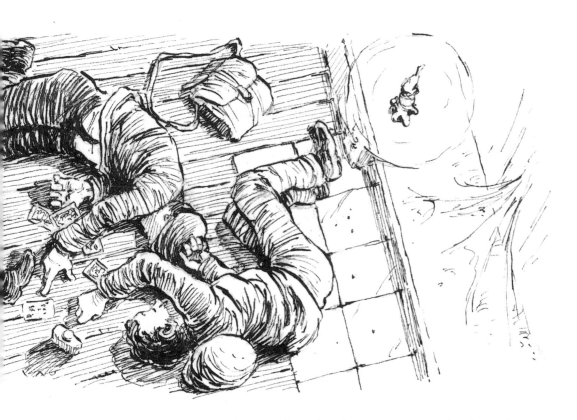

unrest. He tried to whistle, but his lips were parched, and in a mechanical fashion he stooped, and began to pick up the cards which littered the floor.

He stopped once or twice and stood with bent head listening. The unrest outside seemed to increase; a loud creaking sounded from the stairs.

"Who is there?" he cried loudly.

The creaking ceased. He crossed to the door, and, flinging it open, strode out into the corridor. As he walked his fears left him suddenly.

"Come on!" he cried, with a low laugh. "All of you! All of you! Show your faces — your infernal ugly faces! Don't skulk!"

He laughed again and walked on; and the heap in the fireplace put out its head tortoise fashion and listened in horror to the retreating footsteps. Not until they had become inaudible in the distance did the listener's features relax.

"Good Lord, Lester, we've driven him mad," he said, in a frightened whisper. "We must go after him."

There was no reply. Meagle sprang to his feet.

"Do you hear?" he cried. "Stop your fooling now; this is serious. *White! Lester!* Do you hear?"

He bent and surveyed them in angry bewilderment. "All right," he said, in a trembling voice. "You won't frighten me, you know."

He turned away and walked with exaggerated carelessness in the direction of the door. He even went outside and peeped through the crack, but the sleepers did not stir. He glanced into the blackness behind, and then came hastily into the room again.

He stood for a few seconds regarding them. The stillness in the house was horrible; he could not even hear them breathe. With a sudden resolution he snatched the candle from the mantelpiece and held the flame to White's finger. Then as he reeled back stupefied, the footsteps again became audible.

He stood with the candle in his shaking hand, listening. He heard them ascending the farther staircase, but they stopped suddenly as he went to the door. He walked a little way along the passage, and they went scurrying down the stairs and then at a jog-trot along the corridor below. He went back to the main staircase, and they ceased again.

For a time he hung over the balusters, listening and trying to pierce the blackness below; then slowly, step by step, he made his way downstairs, and, holding the candle above his head, peered about him.

"Barnes!" he called. "Where are you?"

Shaking with fright, he made his way along the passage, and summoning up all his courage, pushed open doors and gazed fearfully into empty rooms. Then, quite suddenly, he heard the footsteps in front of him.

He followed slowly for fear of extinguishing the candle, until they led him at last into a vast bare kitchen, with damp walls and a broken floor. In front of him a door leading into an inside room had just closed. He ran towards it and flung it open, and a cold air blew out the candle. He stood aghast.

"Barnes!" he cried again. "Don't be afraid! It is I — Meagle!"

There was no answer. He stood gazing into the darkness, and all the time the idea of something close at hand watching was upon him. Then suddenly the steps broke out overhead again.

He drew back hastily, and passing through the kitchen groped his way along the narrow passages. He could now see better in the darkness, and finding himself at last at the foot of the staircase, began to ascend it noiselessly. He reached the landing just in time to see a figure disappear round the angle of a wall. Still careful to make no noise, he followed the sound of the steps until they led him to the top floor, and he cornered the chase at the end of a short passage.

"Barnes!" he whispered. "Barnes!"

Something stirred in the darkness. A small circular window at the end of the passage just softened the blackness and revealed the dim outlines of a motionless figure. Meagle, in place of advancing, stood almost as still as a sudden horrible doubt took possession of him. With his eyes fixed on the shape in front he fell back slowly, and, as it advanced upon him, burst into a terrible cry.

"Barnes! For God's sake! Is it *you*?"

The echoes of his voice left the air quivering, but the figure before him paid no heed. For a moment he tried to brace his courage up to endure its approach, then with a smothered cry he turned and fled.

The passages wound like a maze, and he threaded them blindly in a vain search for the stairs. If he could get down and open the hall door. . . .

He caught his breath in a sob; the steps had begun again. At a lumbering trot they clattered up and down the bare passages, in and out, up and down, as though in search of him. He stood appalled, and then as they drew near entered a small room and stood behind the door as they rushed by. He came out and ran swiftly and noiselessly in the other direction, and in a moment the steps were after him. He found the long corridor and raced along it at top speed. The stairs he knew were at the end, and with the steps close behind he descended them in blind haste. The steps gained on him, and he shrank to the side to let them pass, still continuing his headlong flight. Then suddenly he seemed to slip off the earth into space.

Lester awoke in the morning to find the sunshine streaming into the room, and White sitting up and regarding with some perplexity a badly blistered finger.

"Where are the others?" inquired Lester.

"Gone, I suppose," said White. "We must have been asleep."

Lester arose, and, stretching his stiffened limbs, dusted his clothes with his hands and went out into the corridor. White followed. At the noise of their approach a figure which had been lying asleep at the other end sat up and revealed the face of Barnes. "Why, I've been asleep," he said, in surprise. "I don't remember coming here. How did I get here?"

"Nice place to come for a nap," said Lester severely, as he pointed to the gap in the balusters. "Look there! Another yard and where would you have been?"

He walked carelessly to the edge and looked over. In response to his startled cry the others drew near, and all three stood staring at the dead man below.

The Wendigo

THEODORE ROOSEVELT

Frontiersmen are not, as a rule, apt to be very superstitious. They lead lives too hard and practical, and have too little imagination in things spiritual and supernatural. I have heard but few ghost stories while living on the frontier, and these few were of a perfectly commonplace and conventional type.

But I once listened to a goblin story which rather impressed me. It was told by a grizzled, weather-beaten old mountain hunter, named Bauman, who was born and had passed all his life on the frontier. He must have believed what he said, for he could hardly repress a shudder at certain points of the tale; but he was of German ancestry, and in childhood had doubtless been saturated with all kinds of ghost and goblin lore, so that many fearsome superstitions were latent in his mind; besides, he knew well the stories told by the Indian medicine men in their winter camps, of the snow-walkers, and the specters, and the formless evil beings that haunt the forest depths, and dog and waylay the lonely wanderer who after nightfall passes through the regions where they lurk. . . .

When the event occurred, Bauman was still a young man, and was trapping with a partner among the mountains dividing the forks of Salmon from the head of Wisdom River. Not having had much luck he and his partner determined to go up into a particularly wild and lonely pass through which ran a small stream said to contain many beaver. The pass had an evil reputation, because the year before a solitary hunter who had wandered into it was there slain, seemingly by a wild beast, the half-eaten remains being afterwards found by some mining prospectors who had passed his camp only the night before.

The memory of this event, however, weighed very lightly with the two trappers, who were as adventurous and hardy as others of their kind. They took their two lean mountain ponies to the foot of the pass, where they left them in an open beaver meadow, the rocky timberclad ground being from thence onwards impracticable for horses. They then struck out on foot through the vast, gloomy forest, and in about four hours, reached a little open glade where they concluded to camp, as signs of game were plenty.

There was still an hour or two of daylight left; and after building brush lean-to and throwing down and opening their packs, they started up stream. The country was very dense and hard to travel through, as there was much down timber, although here and there the somber woodland was broken by small glades of mountain grass.

At dusk, they again reached camp. The glade in which it was pitched was not many yards wide, the tall, close-set pines and firs rising round it like a wall. On one side, was a little stream, beyond which rose the steep mountain-slopes, covered with the unbroken growth of the evergreen forest.

They were surprised to find that during their short absence, something, apparently a bear, had visited camp, and had rummaged about among their things, scattering the contents of their packs, and in sheer wantonness destroying their lean-to.

The footprints of the beast were quite plain but at first they paid no particular heed to them, busying themselves with rebuilding the lean-to, laying out their beds and stores, and lighting the fire.

While Bauman was making ready supper, it being already dark, his companion began to examine the tracks more closely, and soon took a brand from the fire to follow them up, where the intruder had walked along a game trail after leaving the camp. When the brand flickered out, he returned and took another, repeating his inspection of the footprints very closely. Coming back to the fire, he stood by it a minute or two, peering out into the darkness, and suddenly remarked: "Bauman, that bear has been walking on two legs." Bauman laughed at this, but his partner insisted that he was right; and upon again examining the tracks with a torch, they certainly did seem to be made by but two paws, or feet. However, it was too dark to make sure. After discussing whether the footprints could possibly be those of a human being, and coming to the conclusion that they could not be, the two men rolled up in their blankets, and went to sleep under the lean-to.

At midnight, Bauman was awakened by some noise, and sat up in his blankets. As he did so, his nostrils were struck by a strong, wild-beast odor, and he caught the loom of a great body in the darkness at the mouth of the lean-to. Grasping his rifle, he fired at the vague, threatening shadow, but must have missed; for immediately afterwards he heard the smashing of the underwood as the thing, whatever it was, rushed off into the impenetrable blackness of the forest and the night.

After this the two men slept but little, sitting up by the rekindled fire, but they heard nothing more. In the morning, they started out to look at the few traps they had set the previous evening, and to put out new ones. By an unspoken agreement, they kept together all day, and returned to camp towards evening.

On nearing it they saw, hardly to their astonishment, that the lean-to had been again torn down. The visitor of the preceding day had returned; and in wanton malice had tossed about their camp kit and bedding, and destroyed the shanty. The ground was marked up by its tracks; and on leaving the camp, it had gone along the soft earth by the brook, where the footprints were as plain as if on snow, and, after a careful scrutiny of the trail, it certainly did seem as if, whatever the thing was, it had walked off on but two legs.

The men, thoroughly uneasy, gathered a great heap of dead logs, and kept up a roaring fire throughout the night, one or the other sitting on guard most of the time. About midnight, the thing came down through the forest opposite, across the brook, and stayed there on the hillside for nearly an hour. They could hear the branches crackle as it moved about, and several times it uttered a harsh, grating, long-drawn moan, a peculiarly sinister sound. Yet it did not venture near the fire.

In the morning, the two trappers, after discussing the strange events of the last thirty-six hours, decided that they would shoulder their packs and leave the valley that afternoon. They were the more ready to do this because, in spite of seeing a good deal of game sign, they had caught very little fur. However, it was necessary first to go along the line of their traps and gather them, and this they started out to do.

All the morning, they kept together, picking up trap after trap, each one empty. On first leaving camp, they had the disagreeable sensation of being followed. In the dense spruce thickets, they occasionally heard a branch snap after they had passed; and now and then, there were slight rustling noises among the small pines to one side of them.

At noon, they were back within a couple of miles of camp. In the high bright sunlight, their fears seemed absurd to the two

armed men, accustomed as they were, through long years of
lonely wandering in the wilderness, to face every kind of danger
from man, brute, or element. There were still three beaver traps
to collect from a little pond in a wide ravine nearby. Bauman
volunteered to gather these, and bring them in, while his
companion went ahead to camp and made ready the packs.

On reaching the pond, Bauman found three beaver in the traps,
one of which had been pulled loose and carried into a beaver
house. He took several hours in securing and preparing the beaver,
and when he started homewards he marked with some uneasiness
how low the sun was getting. As he hurried towards camp, under
the tall trees, the silence and desolation of the forest weighed on
him. His feet made no sound on the pine needles, and the slanting
sun rays, striking through among the straight trunks, made a gray
twilight in which objects at a distance glimmer indistinctly. There
was nothing to break the ghostly stillness which, when there is no
breeze, always broods over these sombre primeval forests.

At last, he came to the edge of the little glade where the camp
lay, and shouted as he approached it, but got no answer. The
camp fire had gone out, though the thin blue smoke was still
curling upwards. Near it lay the packs wrapped and arranged. At
first, Bauman could see nobody; nor did he receive an answer to
his call. Stepping forward he again shouted; and as he did so, his
eye fell on the body of his friend, stretched beside the trunk of a
great fallen spruce. Rushing towards it, the horrified trapper
found that the body was still warm, but that the neck was broken,
while there were four great fang marks in the throat.

The footprints of the unknown beast-creature, printed deep in
the soil, told the whole story.

The unfortunate man, having finished his packing, had sat
down on the spruce log with his face to the fire, and his back to the

dense woods, to wait for his companion. While thus waiting, his monstrous assailant, which must have been lurking nearby in the woods, waiting for a chance to catch one of the adventurers unprepared, came silently up from behind, walking with long, noiseless steps, and seemingly still on two legs. Evidently unheard, it reached the man, and broke his neck by wrenching his head back with its forepaws, while it buried its teeth in his throat. It had not eaten the body, but apparently had romped and gambolled round it in uncouth, ferocious glee, occasionally rolling over and over it; and had then fled back into the soundless depths of the woods.

Bauman, utterly unnerved, and believing that the creature with which he had to deal was something either half-human or half-devil, some great goblin-beast, abandoned everything but his rifle, and struck off at speed down the pass, not halting until he reached the beaver meadows where the hobbled ponies were still grazing. Mounting, he rode onwards through the night, until far beyond the reach of pursuit.

Story Credits

"The Devil's Breeches" from *Italian Folktales: Selected and Retold by Italo Calvino*, translation by George Martin. English translation copyright ©1980 by Harcourt Brace Jovanovich, Inc. Used by permission of Harcourt, Inc.

"The Honest Ghost" from *Twelve Great Black Cats*, by Sorche Nic Leodhas. Copyright ©1971 by Jenifer Jill Digby. Used by permission of Penguin Putnam Books for Young Readers.

"The Woodcutter's Wife" from *Truly Grim Tales* by Priscilla Galloway. Copyright ©1995 by Priscilla Galloway. Reprinted with the permission of Stoddart Publishing Co. Limited and Dell Publishing, a division of Random House, Inc.

"The Thing and I" from *Scary Poems For Rotten Kids* by Sean O'Huigin. Copyright ©1982 by Sean O'Huigin.

"Beginning With the Ears" from *Ask the Bones: Scary Stories From Around the World* by Arielle North Olson and Howard Schwartz.